Through Roads Between

AMY LAURENS

OTHER WORKS

Find other works by the author at
http://www.amylaurens.com/books/

SANCTUARY

Where Shadows Rise
Through Roads Between
When Worlds Collide

Through Roads Between

AMY LAURENS

AUSTRALIA

ISBN: 978-0-9945238-1-5

www.inkprintpress.com

National Library of Australia Cataloguing-in-Publication Data
Laurens, Amy 1985 –
Through Roads Between
222 p.
ISBN: 978-0-9945238-1-5
Inkprint Press, Canberra, Australia
      1. Fantasy Fiction 2. Fairies 3. Shadows 4. Juvenile
      Fiction

Summary: The Valley's got a hold on her best friend, and Edge must figure out how to save her.

First Edition: September 2017
Printed in the United States of America.

Cover design © Clare Williams.

For you, because you are worth fighting for.

You are worth saving.

Yes, you.

1

SOMEONE TAPPED LIGHTLY on my bedroom door. Groggy with sleep, I felt about in the dark for my phone. The lock screen told me it was nearly 2am. My pulse kicked. It had to be about Gemma, my best friend. My *sick* best friend. "Come in," I said hoarsely.

Mum crept in, house phone in hand.

"Is Gemma okay?" I asked before she spoke.

"I understand," she said, and it took me a second to realise that she was talking to the phone. She hung up and sat on my bed.

I shifted my legs out of the way and waited, barely breathing. The darkness pressed in around us, heavy, full of secrets and fears.

"Is it really something only you can fix?" she asked me. In the shadows, I watched as she twisted the phone in her hands.

I wriggled over and lay my head against her hip, revelling in the comfort of her choc chip cookies and steel soulprint—the unique sensory aura that all people had, and that I could sense and sometimes manipulate because I was a Road Master. "I don't know if I can fix it," I said truthfully. "But I know the doctors can't. She'll die no matter what they do." My pulse stuttered again. Gemma wasn't going to die. I wouldn't let her. "I need to get her to Sanctuary, I think," I said, referring to the home of the fairies that Gemma and I had the ability to travel to.

Unfortunately, Sanctuary wasn't the only other world in existence. The Valley, known more properly as the Valley of Death, was Sanctuary's opposite; where Sanctuary was based on life magic, the Valley ran on death.

And now it had its shadowy tendrils wrapped firmly around my best friend.

In the waiting night, I pressed my eyes shut, trying to remember exactly what the Valley's connection to Gem had looked like. More or less like Scott? Less. Definitely less.

"And Gemma can't just go there by herself?"

"Mum." I shook my head. "She's sick. Like, really sick. Keep her in the hospital overnight sick, remember?"

Mum shot me a sideways glance that I could read more from the slight shift of her head than any ability to see her eyes in this darkness. "No need to sass me, Emma Tanning. You have to understand how absurd this all is from the outside. If it wasn't for Mrs Caro, or..."

I wondered if she was remembering her brief visit to Sanctuary a couple of weeks ago. I shifted awkwardly. "But you've seen it. You know it's real."

She sighed. "You're sure it's something... magical? That's wrong with her?"

I sniffed. "Of course I'm sure. What did Mrs Caro say?"

"That the doctors can't find anything."

"Exactly. 'Soul being drained by Valley of Death' isn't exactly in the medical textbooks, is it?"

Mum hugged me tight. I squirmed until I could breathe. "Be careful, Edge," Mum told me, giving me one last squeeze.

"Always."

The house creaked in the darkness around us, finally cooling after another hot, summery day.

"Liv?" The door protested briefly as Dad nudged it open.

Cool air from the lounge room's aircon unit followed him in, chilling my arms.

"What's wrong?" he murmured.

"It's Gemma," Mum said softly. "She's getting worse. Maria says they need Emma. To... help."

Help. I had to help her. I'd fixed Scott; surely I could save my best friend too.

"I'm going to drive Emma down now," Mum said as I wriggled out from the covers and crossed the night-still bedroom to find clothes.

"Do you want me to come?" Dad asked.

"It's fine," Mum said. "You have meetings tomorrow. I can stay home if I need to."

I couldn't, though, I thought as I pulled on my jeans. No matter what happened tonight, there was no way I was missing school tomorrow. A certain teenage boy held answers to some very important questions, and I'd get those answers or die trying. He wouldn't even know what hit him.

"I'm ready," I said, interrupting Dad as I straightened out my shirt.

Mum stood, the bed pinging and creaking as she did. "Let me get dressed too."

I waited in the front hallway. Tree shadows rippled through the narrow windows on either side of the door, reaching across the floor tiles, rustling, straining. I stood right where they ended and watched as my toes dipped in and out of darkness.

In and out, in and out. Dark and light, dark and light.

One step in either direction and I could be safe, or drown forever.

"Ready?" Mum said behind me, keys clinking too loudly in the night.

I stepped to the front door, into the shadows. "Ready." *I'm coming, Gemma,* I told her. *I'm coming.*

2

THE MORNING HAD started out uneventfully enough. I'd been away at school camp the whole previous week, and Gemma hadn't. She'd messaged me while I'd been away to say she was sick, but hadn't offered any details.

Seeing her slumped against my laminated blue locker at quarter past eight on a Monday morning, it *looked* like she'd been sick: dark circles under her eyes, brown skin sallow, dark hair uncharacteristically limp, school uniform rumpled. "Should you be here?" I asked.

She shrugged.

I let it drop, and squeezed her tightly, inhaling the summery warmth of her soulprint. Camp had been a long week without my best friend.

A whiff of darkness crossed my road mastery sense. I furrowed my eyebrows, twisting around.

"What's up?" Gem asked, releasing me.

"Nothing." I scanned the crowds around us, but Scott was nowhere to be seen. "I thought I felt something is all."

Gem smiled tiredly, hugging her books.

"How's Sanctuary?" I continued, shoving my bag in my locker and pulling out the books I needed for the first two lessons. "Have the twins grown much?" Sanctuary was the home of the fairies, a world outside our own, and a secret we shared as Travellers, who could harness seed magic to cross between worlds.

"I haven't been over much," she confessed.

Worry twanged in my chest. Gem and I practically lived in Sanctuary, when we didn't have to be at school or doing mundane things like eating dinner and sleeping.

But she continued before I could say anything. "Filibere"—one of the baby unicorn twins—"discovered fire geckoes. It was pretty funny."

I laughed, hoping it would encourage her to describe the incident in more detail as we headed down the hall to roll call.

Gem smiled some more, but didn't elaborate.

I ushered her into the classroom ahead of me and frowned at her back. This lack of her usually-abundant enthusiasm was concerning.

More concerning, however, was the fact that Scott had already arrived and was sitting front and centre in the classroom, displacing Gem and me from our usual seats. There was an empty desk to either side, but everywhere else was full. We exchanged glances and sat next to him, me relieved that at least Gem had thought it was weird too. Whatever was wrong with her, at least she could still recognise Scott Behaving Oddly.

I stared at Scott as I sat, avoiding outright suspicion but still an awful long way from friendly as I scrutinised his blond hair—lacking its usual gel spikes—was everyone sick today?—and the knock-off designer glasses he only wore when he really had to.

Scott and I... I shook my head as the teacher came in, and refocused on the front of the classroom.

Scott still hadn't so much as glanced at me. It had been like this for the last three weeks, which was entirely preferable to the uncomfortable attentions he'd bestowed on me before that, but seriously. I'd saved the guy's life. You'd think he could do more than point-blank ignore me.

And yet. After nearly a month of pretending neither Gem nor I existed, here he was, sitting down the front, where he knew we always sat.

Out of the corner of my eye, I saw Gem trying half-heartedly to get my attention. I leaned back in my chair and raised my eyebrows. She tilted her head pointedly at Scott's back.

I shook my head slightly, glancing at the teacher and trying to look like I was still paying attention.

"Say something," she mouthed.

I rolled my eyes, but nodded. Resettling in my seat, I considered my options.

Mrs Johnston, our roll call teacher (and, coincidentally, our science teacher), was handing around some paperwork. Perfect. I grabbed three copies from her and, gritting my teeth, leaned over, placing two of them on Scott's desk. "Pass one to Gem, will you."

Scott took the papers wordlessly and handed one to Gem. His own copy he lay carefully on the desk in front of him, staring down at it without reading.

I chewed on the inside of my lip. Not what I had been expecting. A cutting remark, a line about doing my work for me, something. Not... nothing. Emptiness. What had happened to his spark? Scott had been pretty quiet around us since the whole Valley-shadows saga, but he'd also tried pretty hard to avoid us. And he'd been his usual attention-seeking self around everyone else, as far as I could tell. This... I had to be honest, it felt like he had something to say but couldn't work up the nerve to do so.

I sighed heavily and leaned toward him. "What's up?"

He shrugged, eyes still on his paperwork.

"No but seriously. I almost thought we had the plague, the way you've been avoiding us. What do you want?"

He cut an angry glance at me, a flickering flame of a thing that lasted a bare instant. "Who says I want anything?"

I leaned back in my seat and tapped the short end of my pages against the plastic desk. It made a pleasing sound, like the papers were far heavier than they looked. "Me. And I've been in your head, so I should know." Oh, that came out *totally* wrong. This time I was the one who avoided eye contact.

It did the trick, though: his stare now bored through the side of my skull instead of his papers. I ignored it as long as I could, then gave in and turned—and winced at the intensity of his gaze. The full weight of his soulprint knocked into me, a sense of vastness—an open mountaintop under glittering stars, a cool night wind, and *distance*—that set my teeth on edge.

"I can't—"

"Can't what?" I asked.

He closed his eyes suddenly, a blink that became a pause that became a struggle as his jaw clenched and twitched.

Just tell me. Whatever it is, just tell me and get it over with. I shrugged away nervous tension.

Visiting Sanctuary was supposed to be mildly addictive; the feelings of peace and calm it induced released hormones in the brain, causing visitors to want to seek out the experience again and again and again. Probably, the Valley had some way of enticing its followers to return too—and knowing the Valley, which utilised the power of death instead of the power of life, it wouldn't be as kind as Sanctuary. I'd have to keep a watch on Scott.

Eyes still closed, Scott raised his hand.

"Yes, Mister Harden?"

"Bathroom?" he said, gruffer than usual but also less arrogant, and therefore somehow nicer.

Mrs Johnson nodded from the side of the room where she crouched, discussing something with another student. "Hurry up."

His chair scraped backward, the floor screeching in protest, and Scott left.

It was only then that I noticed Gem was slumped forward, one cheek pressed against the cool desk, staring vacantly out the window. Leaning over Scott's empty chair, I put my hand on her shoulder, bizarrely relieved that it still felt warm. "Gem?"

She didn't move.

"Hello? Gemma?" I said, ducking down to peer closely at her face. She stared some more, utterly ignoring me.

I poked her. Still nothing.

Panicked adrenalin flooded my stomach. "Come on, Gemma," I said. "Come back to me." I closed my eyes and let my road mastery senses take over; the world became overlaid with the multi-sensory soulprints of everyone within fifty metres. I narrowed my focus toward Gem—and abruptly, she fell out of her seat.

The girl next to her screamed and Mrs Johnston appeared as if by magic. "Move back," she commanded as students crowded in to see what had happened.

I stayed in my seat. There'd been something, just as she'd fallen, something in her soulprint...

Ah. There. That was what I'd sensed just now—and this morning when I'd first seen her. I swallowed hard, pushing down nauseated fear, and opened my eyes.

Mrs Johnston performed quick checks for breathing and a pulse before rocking back on her heels, some of the tension in her face and shoulders draining away. "Rahim." She pointed at one of the boys at the back of the crowd. "Go to the office right away. Tell them we need an ambulance. Go!"

Ambulance? *Please let Gem be okay. Please.*

The boy disappeared out of the classroom door. Moments later, Gem groaned, shifting on the floor.

My heart skittered and I remembered how to breathe. Slowly, I released my white-knuckled grip on the desk.

Her eyes rolled open. "Wha..." She squeezed her eyes tight then blinked rapidly.

"Hush," Mrs Johnston soothed. "Just stay where you are. I think it's best if you don't move for now."

Students at the back of the room shuffled aside as the school nurse bustled into the room. "Is she breathing? Is she conscious yet?" she shot at Mrs Johnston, who promptly filled her in on what had happened. The nurse nodded emphatically. "Good. Tracey's calling the ambulance. They should be here shortly, but it looks like it was just an absence seizure."

On the floor, Gemma rolled to one side.

"Should she be doing that?" Mrs Johnston asked.

I leaned forward, perching right on the edge of my seat. *Let her be okay.*

The nurse crouched near Gemma. "Do you hurt anywhere? Can you feel your toes and fingers?"

Gemma scowled. "I'm fine," she said. "I must have fallen asleep or something. My shoulder hurts where I landed on it, but I'm fine."

Gem's sassy attitude dispelled a little of my tension—but not all of it. Not with her soulprint... like *that*.

The nurse allowed her to sit before checking her eyes carefully with her pen torch. "I don't *think* you have a concussion," she said, "but I'd rather you stayed down on the floor until the paramedics get here." Gemma opened her mouth to protest, but the nurse cut her off. "Hush now. You just sit tight. They'll be here soon. How much longer till the first lesson?" That was to Mrs Johnston.

"A minute," Mrs Johnston replied, glancing at the classroom clock.

Around us, students began to pack up their belongings surreptitiously. I clutched mine to my chest, hoping Mrs Johnston wasn't planning on kicking me out. I wasn't budging from this room.

"And I suppose there's a class in here next?" the nurse continued.

Mrs Johnston nodded. "But they can wait in the hallway for a bit."

"Good. The ambulance won't be long."

The rest of the students filed out as the bell went, eyeing Gem as they passed. I waited until they'd all gone, then sat down on the floor.

"Don't you have class?" Mrs Johnston said, raising an eyebrow.

"Please." I hugged my books tighter. "Just for a minute."

Mrs Johnston sighed. She turned and dug through her own things on the teacher's desk, then handed me a signed late slip. "I've got to go," she told the nurse.

The nurse nodded. "I'll stay. It's fine."

Mrs Johnston left, locking the door behind her.

"Maybe you'd better lie back down," the nurse told Gemma. "Just in case."

I patted my knee, and Gemma lay down with her head in my lap. I waited until the nurse settled herself by the doorway, ready to tell the next teacher that their class would have to wait for a bit, then leaned over Gemma.

"I know what's wrong," I whispered.

She stared up at me, eyes glassy with tears. "Edge," she whispered back. "I'm so sorry."

I hugged her awkwardly. "I'll keep you safe," I promised. "It's going to be okay."

3

VOICES MURMURED OUTSIDE in the hall, but in the classroom it was dim and quiet. Satisfied that Gemma wasn't going to lose consciousness again in the next three seconds, I closed my eyes.

Her soulprint (twinkling diamonds in a sky of midnight velvet, plus a high-pitched, barely-audible whirring that made me feel like I was on the edge of remembering something important) shone in the darkness behind my eyes. But there, right at one corner, a black thread grew, stretching away into the distance—and it stank of fetid water and overripe fruit.

"I can feel it," she said quietly. "The Valley. All the time, I can feel it, clawing away at me, tempting me. All the time. It's driving me mad. I thought it would get better after a while, but it's not. It's getting stronger."

I chewed the inside of my lip, weighing our options. "Does your mum know?"

She half shrugged. "I don't want to worry her."

"Oh, you're right: worrying that her daughter feels like the shadow-spawning home of all death and destruction is getting stronger would be *totally* overreacting!" I cut my gaze over to the nurse by the door and lowered my voice. "Yeah. No one needs to worry about *that*."

Gemma's face stilled completely. "I didn't mean it like that."

I let my breath out in a rush of sound. "I know. But you should still probably tell someone."

"I am," she muttered against her hands. "I'm telling you."

"Someone responsible."

She ignored me, and I sighed. The nurse cracked the door open, letting in the chatter of the students. I closed my eyes and let it wash over me, white noise to drown out my thoughts. Everything was going to be fine. I'd saved Scott, and I'd save Gemma too. She'd be just fine.

"The Valley's getting stronger again," Gem said softly.

I scowled. Scott had definitely seemed like he'd wanted to tell me something. "If he's been messing around in the Valley again, I swear, I'll create some more shadows just for him."

Gem stared wide-eyed up at me. "Scott?"

The nurse's soft shadow crossed my lap right at that moment and I flinched. "Okay. Sorry," I told whatever power-of-the-world might be listening. "I didn't mean it and I won't feed anyone to the shadows, including Scott." It had been nearly three weeks, but sudden shadows still made me jumpy, and occasionally I had nightmares of being chased and devoured by darkness.

Of course, it beat nightmares about a dead and bloodied girl called Georgia, who looked uncannily like my sister Anna—the reason we'd moved to Nowra in the first place. Dad had testified against a prominent crime lord and—shockingly enough—the gang hadn't taken it so well. The girl, Georgia, caught the same train home as Anna and, if you didn't know the school uniforms well, you could easily mistake Georgia for Anna. Someone had, and Georgia was found dead in the bathroom at the train station.

Minor correction: *I* found her dead.

And yet, my experience with the shadows in the Valley had terrified me enough that they'd replaced finding a dead body in my nightmares. What more needed to be said?

It occurred to me that Gemma hadn't responded. I glanced down, and stiffened. She was staring sightlessly again.

"Um, excuse me?" My heart pounded as I tried to get the nurse's attention.

But she had her head outside the classroom, talking rapidly to someone.

"Excuse me?" I said, louder.

The nurse pulled the door open all the way, and two paramedics strode in.

"I think she's unconscious again," I said, willing my voice to stay level.

They crouched beside me immediately. "Thanks. We'll take it from here."

And before I could do more than blink, I'd been moved gently aside. The paramedics loaded Gem onto a stretcher, popped it up to full height, and wheeled her from the room.

I clutched my books over the nausea in my stomach, willing myself to forget the stench of the Valley as it left the room with my best friend. I tried to pretend my eyes weren't shining with tears.

"Haven't you got class now?" the nurse said, not unkindly.

I inhaled deeply, nodding, not quite ready to trust my voice again.

I forced myself to loosen my shoulders and exhaled firmly. If the Valley was getting stronger, I'd talk to Aphros—Sanctuary's unicorn—and we'd send it back where it came from. We'd done it before. If we needed to, we could do it again.

I stood up. Everything would be just fine.

I'd caught the bus to the hospital as soon as school had finished, texting Mum to let her know what had happened, and Anna to let her know I wouldn't be on the normal school bus home.

I cleared my throat outside the hospital curtains before peering inside. Mrs Caro smiled at me over a worn magazine, though her eyes remained tight. She tilted her head toward the bed where Gem lay.

I slumped. Black circles smudged Gem's eyes, her dark hair fanning across the pillows like a frame for her too-pale face.

"Sleeping," Mrs Caro said unnecessarily.

I hesitated, half in, half out. "Should I go?" I needed to tell her about the Valley, but if she needed me to go, if she'd had enough trauma for one day...

My hands fisted involuntarily, responding to the cloud of shadows I could sense hovering over Gem's bed.

"Don't be silly," Mrs Caro said. She gave another tight smile. "Did you know the doctors can't find anything wrong with her?"

I shifted uneasily. "They won't."

Mrs Caro's gaze sharpened. "Why not?"

I gripped the straps of my school bag with white knuckles. "It's the Valley." Adrenalin spiked as I remembered being alone in the soundless, sightless dark of the Valley's sinkhole—and then the glowing pillar of light that was the Valley's magic made conscious appearing ahead of me.

It had offered me the world, too, the power to make everything right and keep all my loved ones safe forever and ever. I'd only escaped because Aphros, Sanctuary's unicorn, had sent her soulprint to interrupt the conversation.

Gemma hadn't been so lucky. She'd agreed to the light's bargain—and even though she'd renounced it later, it looked like the Valley was here to collect its payment regardless.

She nodded once, decisively. "Unsurprising."

"It's..." I flicked a nervous glance at Gem. "It's getting stronger. Fast."

"Do you know why?"

I shook my head.

Mrs Caro closed her eyes and leaned back against the wall.

Somewhere beyond the blue curtains, heart rate monitors bipped and nurses chattered, rustling their paperwork and shuffling their footsteps.

"I'm sorry," I whispered.

Mrs Caro's eyes blinked open, wide with surprise. "Sorry? Oh, Emma. You have nothing to be sorry for. Thank you for letting me know what the problem really is. Who knows how long Gemma might have tried to hide it."

She reached out and I let her hug me. "It's going to be okay, isn't it?" I said when she let me go.

She held me by the shoulders. "I don't know. But Aphros will."

I nodded. "But she'll probably have to see Gemma in person," I said. That wasn't a bad thing, though; exposing Gemma to the calming magic of Sanctuary might actually be helpful. "What's the earliest we could get Gemma there?"

"The doctors want to look into the seizures. They have her booked in for an MRI, but I'm not sure they'll find anything, because if you're right, there's nothing for modern medicine to find. I suppose it'll have to be tomorrow afternoon. I can't imagine being able to sneak her out before that—although if it's very desperate I could take her out against medical orders. What do you think? Will that be necessary?"

I bit my lip and tried to compare the strength of the Valley's bond with Gemma now compared to this morning, trying to calculate how fast it might be growing. "Tomorrow morning would be better," I said. The connection lurked at the edge of my awareness constantly, like a hungry predator that kept my teeth on edge.

Mrs Caro sighed. "And tonight would be even more preferable. Still." She picked up the magazine again. "Keep your phone on you. I'll let you know when we're out and heading to Sanctuary."

I nodded. "Call me anytime," I said. "I'll sneak out if I have to."

Mrs Caro peered sternly at me over the magazine. "Edge, dear, there may be no one else on the planet who can help me save my daughter right now, but I'm not going to drag you away from bed in the middle of the night without your parents' permission. You go home now and rest," she continued over my protests. "I'll call the house if it's really urgent. I think," she said, glancing at Gemma, "that it will not be necessary."

I gave her a half smile. "I hope so too, Mrs Caro. I hope so too."

4

WHICH LED TO the here and now, sitting in a car, staring out the window as dark houses flashed past, normal people curled up asleep, warm and safe and oblivious to the shadows. A few weeks ago, I'd been just like them, oblivious to the horrors of the night.

Well. Not strictly true. I'd been under witness protection and infinitely aware of the *human* horrors of the night, but that was different.

I snorted softly. Very different. Back then, I'd been helpless. The shadows might be scarier than any mobster, but I'd beaten them once, and I'd do it again. My hands clenched in my lap as we turned over the bridge. This time, I wasn't helpless. This time, I could fight back.

The red and green lights of the channel winked at me in the darkness, the dim night lights of the town reflecting off the river. In the dark, there was no way of telling how fast the river flowed, or where the treacherous currents were—except the lights, red and green, steadfast sentinels in the night. There was a way through this nightmare. I just had to find it.

We pulled off the main road toward the hospital and my stomach clenched.

"Okay?" Mum asked.

I nodded curtly.

A moment later, we pulled into the hospital's carpark, gravel crunching under the tyres. I sat still for a moment, staring at the fluorescent lights of the entrance.

"You coming?" Mum asked from outside the car, peering back in at me.

"Yeah." I couldn't feel the Valley from here, not really—neither my road mastery nor the Valley's connection with Gemma were that strong—but I knew what I'd feel as soon as I walked in: queasy, oily stagnant-water stench, rotten fruit, fear.

I unbuckled my belt. Worse, Mrs Caro had said. How much worse? How much worse did it have to be before she'd call me in the middle of the night?

I set my shoulders, clenched my hands at my sides, and strode toward the hospital.

Inside, I stopped dead as Mum pushed the curtains of Gemma's bed area aside; the sight of the dark shadows wreathing Gemma's soulprint felt like a physical punch to the gut.

"What do you think?" Mrs Caro asked me, face pinched and tight.

I shook my arms briskly and exhaled, forcing my road mastery down to a mere trickle so the shadows felt less overwhelming. "You were right to call me," I said. "The connection's a lot stronger. We need to get her to Sanctuary right away."

She nodded, lips pursed. "I thought so. Thank you for coming. Thank you for bringing her," she added, turning to Mum.

I caught a brief glimpse of Mum's face, odd expression twisting her features. I ignored it, and took Gemma's hand as she lay barely conscious.

"It's fine," Mum replied. "This is really something only Emma can fix?"

Mrs Caro's lips stretched into a sad smile. "If anyone can."

"How are we going to do this?" I said, aware that I might be interrupting and not really caring. "She doesn't look like she can walk far."

"She can't," Mrs Caro agreed, joining me at the bedside. "But I can probably find a wheelchair to get her to the car."

I nodded. "Do it."

Mrs Caro left. I felt Mum's eyes on me again, and realised the reason for the odd expression: nowhere else in my life was I permitted to treat an adult as an equal like this. "I'm not being rude," I noted, without looking at her.

"I know," she replied. "It's just... unusual. You're barely thirteen, and Maria treats you like you're in charge."

That's because I am, I didn't say. "Road mastery isn't common," I said instead. "According to the fairies, there are only a handful of people with it. And most of them can't do what I can."

"Like what?"

I glanced at Mum. We'd had plenty of opportunities to discuss this in the last couple of weeks, and she wanted to discuss it here, now?

She met my eye levelly. Oh. A distraction, perhaps?

I gave her a brittle smile and leaned my butt on the edge of Gemma's bed so I could face her. "I can sense people's soulprints," I said. "Like... a multi-sensory trail unique to each person. It's strongest right where they are at the time, of course, but I can see where people have been recently, or if there's somewhere they go a lot, I can usually pick that up as well."

"But why call it *road* mastery then? It doesn't seem to have much to do with roads."

"I..." I closed my mouth and bunched my lips to one side. "I don't know. I can see the paths people travel, I guess? That's like roads, right?"

She shrugged, pouting her bottom lip in a 'beats me' expression. "Doesn't seem like the most obvious name."

"I guess not," I said, eyes on Gemma. She hadn't moved since we'd arrived, although she was breathing the deep breaths of sleep now rather than seeming to fight for air. I really hoped she was going to be okay.

"You said you can sense where someone's been, but only for a little while. How long?"

"Depends."

"On what?"

"A lot of things. How many other people are around. How many other people have crossed over the trail. How often the person uses that route. Those are the main things." I thought of our house, layered with months and months of usage. "The house, I can sense all of you as soon as I open the door. Before, even. Our Melbourne house?"

We'd lived there for ten years. Mum nodded.

"I could sense you all turning into the street. Not that I knew that's what I was sensing."

I remembered visiting Sanctuary for the first time with Gemma and the fairy Quoise, and learning that I was a Road Master. In Sanctuary, my talents were a lot stronger, helped by Sanctuary's magic, but there had been some sort of crystallising effect that had transferred over to this world: previously, I'd had a bunch of vague sensations attached to people I knew well or dealt with regularly, but nothing I could consciously pick out. I could tell when someone I was close to approached before I saw them, and sometimes people would irritate me or give me the creeps for no apparent reason.

After visiting Sanctuary, everything became sharper: instead of just vague sensations, I could describe people's soulprints—although admittedly in terms that often made no sense to other people. I could pick out individual soulprints and follow trails, much like I imagined scent hounds could do. "About fifty metres or so," I said.

Mum wrinkled her eyebrows.

"Your next question was going to be, 'How far away can you sense someone?' The answer is, about fifty metres or so. Unless, like I said, it's a place the person visits a lot and there's a sort of residual sense of their soulprint there."

Mum glanced at the luridly-lit hospital ward. "Must be a lot of soulprints flying around here."

Innocent enough words, but something in the way she said it made me narrow my eyes. "Yes. Lots. Why do you say that?"

She shrugged, still peering around. "I just... It feels crowded in here. Noisy. There are lots of people, so I assume you can see lots of soulprints, right?"

Noisy? Apart from the hum of machinery and the beeps of monitors, the place was almost silent. I shifted forward, squinting one eye at her more than the other. "Mum, are you a Road Master?"

She laughed and rubbed at her arms.

"No, I'm serious," I said. "It often runs in families. Gemma's family has time mastery. Mrs Caro's pretty good, she can get us back up to a couple of hours before we even left. Gemma's mastery is weaker, but it's good enough to make sure we always get back on time."

Mum frowned. "How would I know? I can't do anything like you say you can, with seeing soulprints and things like that."

"I couldn't before I went to Sanctuary, not properly."

"I've been to Sanctuary, and nothing changed." She stared at her hands, suddenly motionless in her lap, and for the first time I realised that maybe she *wanted* to be able to join the magic of Sanctuary.

I guess it made sense. It seemed like most people wanted to believe that magic was real, and Mum *knew* it was real, but couldn't join in. That... had to suck, actually.

"Are you *sure* nothing changed?" I asked, watching her carefully. She shifted as she thought; there was definitely something she wasn't telling me. "Nothing at all?"

She shifted her weight again, staring at her hands a moment longer before meeting my eye. "Sometimes... I think I hear something when your dad comes into the room. And Anna. And when you're around..."

"Stop!" I said, holding my hands up. She looked startled; I smiled to soften my tone. "We're not supposed to know what our own soulprints look like."

She blinked. "Why not? It would make sense that you couldn't *sense* your own, but why can't you even know what it is?"

"...I don't actually know," I said. "Quoise told me it's one of the fairies' rules." Like ignoring the shadows. Hmm. "But seriously, you hear something around Dad and Anna?" I grinned.

She squirmed, looking totally out of character. "I'm not a hundred per cent sure," she said. "I can't hear it all the time. Just... I don't know. Would I be more certain if it was actually something like what you can do?"

I shrugged. "Not necessarily. I didn't know until Sanctuary, remember. Does Anna sound like a faint clacking? Like keyboard keys or something?"

Mum's face lit up. "Yes! That's exactly it! I would never have been able to tell you that, but you're right. It's exactly like keys clacking, only very faint, like they're several rooms away and I can only catch them when the conditions are just right." She tilted her head like she was listening. "I can hear you now," she said softly. "It's a pity you can't."

My stomach jolted. What would I hear if I could hear my own soulprint? What did it even mean that part of my soulprint was a sound? Soulprints were an unpredictable combination of the senses, and usually only two or three of them. Gemma was an image—twinkling stars—a sound—a high-pitched, mildly irritating whirr—and a texture—dark velvet. Mum was two smells—fresh-baked chocolate chip cookies and steel—and the feeling of a smooth, polished steel rod.

I always took that to mean that Gemma was a little annoying but super nice once you got to know her, and a bit obsessed with glamour. Mum was homey and the basic personification of comfort, with a backbone of steel determination.

"I guess that's conclusive then," I said. "You're a Road Master, Mum. Congratulations." I smiled warmly.

She smiled back before wrinkling her brow. "Then why can't I cross to Sanctuary too?"

"The two things don't go together. Separate talents. But," I frowned too, "travelling also tends to run in families. I don't know. I'll have to ask Quoise."

Mum shrugged. "Maybe you get the travelling from your dad."

Now there was a thought: Dad in Sanctuary.

Before I could meditate on it further, a rolling, wheeling, tick-tick-tick drew nearer. Mrs Caro pushed back the curtain and snuck inside, pushing a worn grey wheelchair. "Are we ready?" she said furtively. "They might notice this missing soon."

I looked at Gem, lying in the bed, and opened my road mastery out a fraction wider again. I recoiled. "Yeah," I said, stifling the need to brush the filthy magic off me. "We need to go."

5

WE MADE IT to the cars without a fuss, and from there it was less than ten minutes back to our house—the closest place to the glade by the creek where we could cross to Sanctuary. Mum had pointed out that technically, Lynburn Avenue was closer, but Mrs Caro and I had quickly shut that idea down.

"The Valley crossing is on that side of the creek," I'd explained. "And trust me, we don't want Gemma any closer to the Valley than we can help right now." I'd side-eyed the growing cord of blackness attached to her soulprint, now as thick as three of my fingers.

So we'd parked outside our house, and now were contemplating how best to get Gemma to the glade.

She'd roused when we'd moved her to the wheelchair, and as Mum and I headed to the Caro's car in the driveway behind us, I could hear Gem's voice. My pulse skipped with relief.

"You can't carry me the whole way there," she was saying to Mrs Caro.

"And you can't walk. You're barely able to sit."

True enough; we'd put the passenger seat back as far as we safely could, and despite her protestations, Gem couldn't even sit up by herself.

I popped her door open and leaned in to hug her gently. "How are you feeling?"

"Useless." She turned her face away, but not before I saw the tears spill over. "And stupid, and a complete waste of space."

I hugged her again, awkwardly, crouching and laying my head against her side. "You're not useless," I told her. "Or a waste of space. And you're not even stupid."

"I am," she whispered as Mrs Caro got out. "If I wasn't stupid, the Valley would never have tricked me in the first place."

"It's not your fault, Gem."

"Pretty sure it is, actually," she whispered, and despite everything, I smiled for a second, because just for that one sentence she sounded like herself.

"Okay," I allowed. "Maybe it is. But we all still love you a lot, Gem. We're not going to abandon you because you made one dumb choice."

She didn't answer, her whole body quivering. I hugged her tight.

Someone tapped me on the shoulder—Mum, motioning me aside. I stretched upright, knees protesting as blood flowed back to my legs.

Mum and Mrs Caro had rigged a stretcher of sorts between them using some rakes and a tarp. They loaded Gemma on, locked the cars, and we set off down the street. I led the way, my phone's torch shining brightly.

After a tense few minutes navigating the stairs through the boulders, we reached the bottom. In daylight, I'd be able to see the creek in front of us, but at night there was only an inky blackness.

I tripped on Mum's foot as I tried to get in front of them again to light the way. "Sorry."

"Spooky, isn't it?" Mum said quietly.

"What? No. It's just dark." Spooky was the Valley shadows.

Crickets chirped and some other sort of insect whirred, and something rustled in the branches above us. We walked on in silence.

"Stop here," Mrs Caro said breathily as we neared the place where we had to turn off the path. She and Mum lay Gem's stretcher carefully on the ground. "Where's the easiest way in?"

I shone my torchlight into the trees, searching for the clearest way (we made a point of entering through a different place each time, trying to avoid making an obvious tunnel). "In there," I said after a moment, shining my light a little to the left.

Mrs Caro nodded. "Lead on."

I led the way into the bushes. They protested, scratching and scraping, reminding me of my first desperate run through the Valley when the trees had come to life and tried to stop me from leaving.

I took a deep breath. No Valley here.

The back of my neck prickled.

I opened up my road mastery and cringed. "We'd better hurry," I said. The shadows around Gemma's soulprint were massing; the entrance to the Valley just across the creek must be calling to them.

"Is she getting worse?" Mrs Caro asked, breathless and sharp.

"No," I said, snapping a branch and ducking into the little open space by the creek that we called the glade. "But the shadows are."

"Shadows?" Mum asked.

"Again?" said Mrs Caro.

I shook my head. "No. They aren't..." I struggled for the right words. "Last time," I said, turning to Mum, "the Valley sent out shadows that tried to lure people in for it. Food, kind of."

Kind of? Exactly. Chills ran down my back as I remembered the shadows' words: *Eat, eat your soul, give us your life, life so sweet, so sweet your blood.* "These aren't like last time," I told Mrs Caro. "They're not as *real*. They're just..." I eyed Gemma uneasily. "Testing."

Mrs Caro's lips still looked concerned.

"Let's just get started," I said. I felt Mum giving me the same odd look she'd given me at the hospital—but I couldn't help it: this time, I really was in charge.

Thankfully, Mrs Caro nodded. "Do you want to do the crossing, or should I?"

"Can I?" I asked, reaching into my pocket for my packet of seeds. I never went anywhere without them these days. "I'm not sure I can carry the stretcher."

Mrs Caro nodded. "Of course."

"Are we ready?" I asked as we clustered around, making sure everyone could touch my free hand. "Gem?" I flicked the torchlight over her to check she was still with us. She stared past me, and for a moment I thought she was about to seize again. Then I realised: she wasn't staring blankly. She was staring into the trees on the other side of the creek—at the main entrance to the Valley. I rubbed away the goosebumps that rose on my arms. I didn't want to know what was going through her head right now.

"Gem," I said gently. "I need your hand."

She didn't move.

Mouth pressed firmly in a thin line, Mrs Caro took one of Gemma's hands in her own, then sandwiched it between hers and mine. Mum laid her hand on top, and it was time. I closed my eyes, shoved my seed-finger as deep into the dirt as it

41

would go, and waited for the tiny spark of magic that happened when a seed took root.

Normally it took a couple of days for a seed to germinate and release its power. Travellers like me and Gem and Mrs Caro, though, could speed things up, making the seed germinate immediately and harnessing its power to cross between worlds. With my eyes still closed, I pictured the Sanctuary alcove in as much detail as I could manage: silvery-green grass tickling beneath my knees, soft ground with a little spring and give, the fresh, clean smell of the breeze, the perpetual pearly twilight of the sky above...

Within a second, the scenery around us shifted and we opened our eyes in Sanctuary. I smiled as the sense of peace that accompanied the transition flooded over me. If anywhere could make Gemma better, Sanctuary could.

Gem, however, didn't seem peaceful at all. She twisted and writhed on the stretcher, moaning under her breath.

I leaned closer.

"Can't stand it..." she mumbled. "Hurts..."

I looked up and met Mrs Caro's eye. "The Lodge?"

She nodded. "The fairies will know what to do."

Mum and Mrs Caro lifted the stretcher once more, and we headed up the grassy slope, past the unicorns' stables, and to the fairies' Lodge, stopping once or twice to give the stretcher-bearers a breather. I offered to switch for a bit, but they both shook their heads determinedly until I gave up asking and led them up the slope in silence.

We headed straight to the front doors of the Lodge. I swung them open, standing awkwardly to the side while Mum and Mrs Caro brought Gemma in.

The cavernous room shimmered and flittered with movement as fairies of all colours and hues made their way through it. Their butterfly wings flashed, some flying in or out of connecting doorways, some hovering by bookshelves that lined the far walls, and some congregating around a lovely hanging garden that served as their reception.

I let the doors fall closed and turned toward the reception desk—and something small and blue zipped in front of my face, forcing me to stop with the stretcher right behind me.

It was Quoise, the fairy assigned to watching over Gemma and me while we were in Sanctuary, and our first point of contact. I opened my mouth to greet her, but she interrupted me, cheeks pale and eyes strained. "You can't be here," she said tightly. "Quick, quick, get outside. Hurry!"

I frowned.

"Quoise," said Mrs Caro firmly, not at all diminished by being still a little out of breath, "Gemma needs help."

"Doesn't matter, doesn't matter!" Quoise muttered, herding us back to the door.

A shout echoed out behind us. "Stop!"

"Pretend you haven't heard," said Quoise. "Don't stop, don't stop!"

Quoise pushed at Mum's shoulder, trying to get her moving again.

Too late. A fairy I hadn't seen before with emerald-green wings and a tiny gold coronet interposed herself between us and the door. She drew herself up to her full height in mid-air—which, although not tall, was still a good palm's width taller than Quoise—and glared at us, white-lipped with outrage. "How *dare* you trespass here!"

We stared.

"I think there's been a mistake," I said slowly. "Gemma's here—"

"Exactly!" the fairy snapped. "*That* is the mistake."

"...for help," I finished lamely.

"Get out," the fairy told Gemma. "If I see you here again, or hear word of you here again, I will personally see to it that your future life, such as it is, will be a misery. I will not allow you to destroy what we have made." The emerald-winged fairy folded her arms over her chest and inclined her head toward the door.

Utterly confused, we exited, with Quoise hovering anxiously behind.

44

"Quoise."

The emerald fairy's tone made me flinch.

"Where are you going?"

"Just... down... Aphros," Quoise stammered. "I'm going to see Aphros, Your Grace."

"See that you do," the emerald fairy commanded. "I don't have to remind you of our rules, do I?"

"N-no, Your Grace," Quoise said.

We exited as fast as we could with the unwieldy stretcher and headed down the slope.

"Your Grace?" I said as we moved out of earshot.

Quoise shrugged, discomfort twisting her features. "She is the Keeper. Sanctuary's leader. Everything we do is done according to her word."

"I didn't realise Sanctuary was a dictatorship."

"It's not like that!" Quoise said, voice strained.

"Quoise," Mrs Caro said in a 'Really?' tone of voice. She seemed less puzzled by the situation, now that I thought about it, and I wondered if she'd run into the Keeper before.

"The Keeper," I said slowly as we walked. "Did she... Did she just ban Gemma from Sanctuary?"

Beside me, Quoise nodded.

"But... why?"

Quoise fluttered along silently.

"It's the Valley, isn't it?" Mum said, looking from Quoise to me and back again.

At the front of the stretcher, Mrs Caro stared resolutely ahead.

Quoise nodded, lip between her teeth. "I'm sorry," she whispered. "There's nothing we can do."

"No." I shook my head. "There has to be something. I can do something." *Surely*.

Quoise shook her own head in response. "Edge, there's nothing. She accepted the Valley's offer, and even though you contained the shadows and destroyed the Valley's avatar, Gem is still bound to it." Quoise touched my cheek. She looked over at Mrs Caro. "I'm so sorry. There's nothing we can do."

6

"WAIT," I SAID as Mrs Caro and Mum began walking again, Gemma moaning as the stretcher shifted and bumped.

"Why?" Mrs Caro said. "You heard Quoise. They won't do anything."

"It isn't 'won't', Maria," Quoise said in equally snappy tones.

"Wait," I said again as my heart raced. The implications of the Keeper's ban echoed around my thoughts. Gemma could never come back to Sanctuary again. "We can't just leave."

Mrs Caro gave me a weary look. "Edge, you heard the Keeper. Gemma's banned. There's nothing else we can do."

Gem twisted, muttering incomprehensibly.

I can do something. I have to try something. Quoise went still in the corner of my vision, and I turned to her abruptly. "What is it?" I demanded. "What aren't you telling us?"

Quoise's wings quivered as she perched on the edge of the stretcher, staring at Gem. We walked onward, nearing the alcove, our feet shushing in the grass.

"Please don't tell them I'm talking to you about this," Quoise said softly.

Shh, shh, shh went our feet.

"The Valley and Sanctuary exist in opposition; just as we fairies can't cross over to the Valley because its magic will destroy us, so too the magic of Sanctuary will eventually destroy Gem. And that's assuming that the Valley doesn't consume her first and use her as a way to destroy Sanctuary. She's dangerous, Edge." She wrapped her arms around her tiny body. "That's why the Keeper banned her. It's for the best."

Mrs Caro shot her a sharp glance.

"But that's rubbish!" I said. "You can't just kick her out of Sanctuary and leave her be! The Valley will consume her, and then she'll come after Sanctuary anyway! This is just like last time, when the fairies wanted to ignore the shadows and pretend they'd go away."

Quoise cut me off with a shake of her head, wings flapping in agitation. "Not all of us were ignoring them."

Mum turned to me. "Can you do anything?"

My chest ached. I *had* told Mum that I could fix Gemma—that's why she'd driven me to the hospital in the middle of the night. But last time, there had been a literal personification of the Valley to fight. I could *see* the Valley's connection to Gemma's soulprint, but I wasn't sure how to detach it. "I don't know what to do. I was hoping the fairies would help me figure it out."

"If anyone can do something, you can," Quoise said softly.

I tossed my head. My eyes were getting scratchy and a headache was threatening; it had to be getting close to four in the morning back home. "I got rid of them last time because I had help from Aphros, and the Valley's power was embodied. A body I could fight against. I didn't actually do anything to the shadows, if you recall."

Still. Maybe Aphros would have an idea. And I wasn't leaving Sanctuary without at least *trying*. I set my jaw. "I need to talk to Aphros."

The mothers exchanged glances. "With or without Gemma?" Mrs Caro asked.

I bit my lip. "With. She'll need to help me manipulate Gemma's soulprint."

Mrs Caro gave her head a brisk jerk. "So we'll have to cause a diversion, then."

"I'll do it," Quoise said, fluttering into the air.

Mrs Caro gestured with her head and Mum helped her put the stretcher down a little way from the crossing point, where a neat little rockery filled one side of the alcove. "Thank you, Quoise," she said, stretching with her hands on her lower back, "but I've got this one. I'm sure you're more than capable of holding the Keeper's attention when necessary, but we all know your principle personality feature is general niceness."

Quoise flapped her wings, cheeks pinking.

"I, on the other hand," Mrs Caro continued, "can be very annoying when I want to be." The smile she gave was all tooth, like a shark.

Mum turned to me. "Would you rather I stayed or went?"

I shrugged. "It doesn't matter."

She grinned, and I caught a glimpse of the steel rod that was an integral part of her soulprint. "In that case, I'll go with Maria. It's been a while since I got to be really annoying."

They left together, hurrying back up the slope like they hadn't just carried a nearly full-grown girl on a stretcher up the same slope and back down it.

"That was revealing," Quoise murmured.

I blinked. "You're telling me," I said, shaking my head a little.

"I'll go get Aphros," Quoise said, stirring herself.

"I can just call her," I said. When we'd banished the shadows last time, I'd stepped into Aphros's soulprint so we could fight together. Since then, we'd maintained a strange sort of connection between us; I could tell where she was, no matter how far away—and if we concentrated, we could talk to each other too.

"If I stay here," Quoise said, "it'll draw attention to your presence. I'll go hang out with the babies," she finished, referring to Aphros's twins, Filibere and Lily.

I nodded, not sad to have a few moments alone to process everything that had happened.

"Back soon." Quoise took off at full pace, a blur in the air. I'd never seen her hurry like that before; I was impressed.

My eyes lost her in Sanctuary's dim twilight and I turned back to Gem, pulse stuttering as I realised her eyes were open. "Hey," I said softly as I perched on a dark grey rock next to the stretcher.

A flame-coloured bush crept from the crevice between my rock and the next, and a trail of white pebbles swirled away to my right. The little rockery was pretty, calming. I wondered if there was something in its design that amplified Sanctuary's calming magic. Maybe not. Pretty things could be soothing too.

Gem blinked up at me.

"How are you feeling?" I asked.

She worked her jaw. "I heard it all," she rasped.

My chest constricted. "I'm sorry."

A pale smile hovered over her features. "You'll fix it," she said simply.

I squeezed her hand. "Yeah."

So much for not making promises I couldn't keep. I didn't have to close my eyes to feel her connection to the Valley, thick as my wrist now, and greasy. I hoped desperately that it was just Sanctuary amplifying my road mastery, and not that the connection had actually strengthened that much since the hospital.

Footsteps rustled in the grass outside the alcove and a white horsey head appeared. "I am sorry," Aphros said as she entered the alcove. "The fairies were following me. I took the roundabout route."

Judging by the slivers of shadow clinging to her mane, the roundabout route involved travelling through the Valley—a smart move, since the fairies couldn't follow her there. She tossed her mane. "Show me."

I moved aside and gestured to Gem.

Aphros recoiled.

"That bad, huh?" I murmured.

She snorted and moved closer. "Help me."

I held my hands out helplessly, wondering exactly what it was I was supposed to do.

She moved parallel to the stretcher, then shifted further so my outstretched hand rested lightly on her flank, stomping a hind foot absently.

Right. That then.

With my hand touching her, she could interact with my road mastery, helping me to direct and control it. I closed my eyes and focused on Gemma's soulprint.

"Hmm."

"Hmm what?" I said, pulse fluttering. "Hmm good or hmm bad?"

She exhaled noisily and shifted her weight. "Just hmm. Quoise said the shadows were massing around her, but they've actually connected themselves with her soulprint."

No duh, I thought, examining the thick cable of darkness that stretched from Gemma's soulprint out toward the Valley.

"That is more serious than Quoise suggested, but I do not think it is insurmountable."

"Come again?"

"I think you can separate Gemma from the Valley."

Relief trilled through my body and I let my arm relax, disconnecting from Aphros's silky side with a feeling like pins and needles.

Aphros swung toward me. "Why did you let go?"

I blinked. "I thought we were done."

"I said you can separate Gemma from the Valley, not that you could do it without killing her."

All the tension that had melted away snapped back into place. "But... I thought..."

Aphros nuzzled my side. "I am not finished. Lend me your hands once more, and let us see what can be done," she said gently.

Apprehensive, I placed my hand on Aphros's neck and turned wide-eyed to look at Gemma.

"Please save her," I whispered to Aphros. I'd lost friends moving here from Melbourne, but it'd turned out they hadn't really been friends at all. Gemma was the first friend I'd had who hadn't tried to make me be someone I wasn't.

"I'm sorry," I told Gem. "I should have tried harder. I should have found you sooner." If only I'd gotten to her earlier when she'd disappeared into the Valley, maybe the shadows wouldn't have sunk their claws into her.

"Aphros," I breathed. Our connection meant I didn't have to speak aloud at all, especially when we were this close, but it felt too serious a thing to ask in silence.

"Mmm?"

"Why didn't you save her? You saved me," I continued, remembering a pillar of mint and gold appearing in the darkness right as I was about to sell my soul to the Valley.

Aphros twitched. "Road mastery," she said simply. "Your soulprint is easier to find, because it quests, always searching outward with your senses. You are easy to find," she repeated. "I did not find Gemma soon enough."

"Oh." My chest felt heavy and tight.

"There," she said, tone shifting toward certainty. "Right there. Can you see, Edge?"

I closed my eyes again and looked. In front of me, Gemma's soulprint stretched and grew; Aphros was directing my vision, zooming me in, something I couldn't do by myself. One day, I'd have to have a good long talk with Aphros about what my road mastery could and couldn't do.

We drew closer and closer to the stretched-out sky of Gemma's soulprint, and I realised as we did that instead of doming out evenly like a velvet blue-black sky, her soulprint seemed to buckle and pull. The cord, I realised: the connection to the Valley was pulling on her soulprint, distorting it. "I see it."

"Look closer," Aphros said, and directed my vision right to the very root of the Valley's fetid, black connection.

Tiny fibres stretched out from the cord, sinking themselves into the warp and weft of Gemma's print. I could see how we might be able to pick them out from her soulprint—but I could see too the wear it would cause. Gemma's soulprint would be permanently weakened there.

"What happens when our soulprints fray?" I asked Aphros quietly.

"It depends on how bad the wear is," she said, equally as quiet. "Sometimes the fray can heal. Sometimes it remains the same, a leak in the owner's energies; they would feel always exhausted, like they are battling against the current. Some-times the fray gets worse."

I swallowed. The fibres from the Valley's cord stretched out a good way into Gemma's soulprint. "But Scott was okay. And we separated him from his connection with the Valley."

"The boy was as good as dead anyway. We tried in desperation. We are all lucky he was strong enough to heal."

Strong enough to heal. I hadn't thought of Scott like that before. "So what can we do?" *Please. Please let there be something we can do.*

"I think," she said carefully, and my vision suddenly blacked.

I blinked, disoriented, before realising Aphros had pulled away.

"I *think* that there is nothing we can do that would not end in irreparable harm."

My stomach sank.

"But..."

"But? But what?" *Don't torment me like this, Aphros,* I sent silently to her.

She snorted, tossing her mane vigorously. *I am not tormenting you. I am trying not to promise things I have no knowledge of.*

Ha. I could definitely identify with that, even if I was doing an abysmal job of avoiding it.

"I do not think we can fix her," she continued aloud. "But there might be some-thing we could do to slow its progress."

"What?" I said. "What could we do?"

"The problem is not the connection, per se. The problem is that the connection is growing, yes?"

"It started as a tiny, thin thread," I said. "And now... Well, you can see how thick it is now. And she's gotten much worse since it has."

Aphros's soft hair rubbed against my fingertips as she nodded. "If we could constrict it somehow, and possibly stretch it out, it would thin."

My pulse sped up. "Like clay," I said. "Roll it out longer and it gets thinner. But how do we roll it?"

"I do not think we can roll it, as you say, but perhaps..." The darkness behind my eyes lit up as Aphros zoomed me off again, directing my road mastery first to the place where the Valley's cord interwove with Gemma's soulprint, and then a little way down the cord itself.

"Lend me your strength."

I didn't exactly understand what she meant, but I could sense her asking for something from my road mastery, like someone holding out their hand for a thing you were carrying. I struggled for a second, wondering how to give her what she seemed to want. Extra power? My road mastery itself? I tried reaching toward her with my road mastery sense, like concentrating hard on an object just out of reach.

A silvery fog extended toward her. Aphros tugged on it gently; I felt it deep inside my head, like she was pulling on my thoughts.

I watched, wondering what she would do with the power she'd taken from me—and then the space around the Valley's cord glimmered, gold and green and silver, and the scent of mint and old roses surrounded me.

The colourful glimmer solidified, and although I couldn't see her precisely, I sensed Aphros working, feeding more power into the glimmer, honing it, shaping it—until at last, a bright gold-and-silver pipe encased the Valley's cord, drawing it out as fine as wire.

"There," Aphros said at last. The vision faded away as she shifted from under my hand. "I think that will hold for at least a few days."

I blinked rapidly, my head reeling a little. Whatever she'd done, Aphros had just drawn a heck of a lot of power from me. I felt spacey and just a little bit unreal.

But beside me, Gem shifted in the stretcher. "Edge?"

I bent down to her, chest lightening. The dark circles under her eyes had faded a little, and her eyes were clear. "How are you feeling?"

"Better," she said. "Not great, but better."

I reached down and hugged her tight, and she half sat up to hug me back. "Thank you," I said over Gemma's back to Aphros.

She inclined her head, but before she could speak, Mum and Mrs Caro raced into the alcove.

"Out!" Mrs Caro said. "Quick, out! Out!"

I stared for a moment, unable to move.

"The fairies!" Mrs Caro said. She and Mum snatched up the stretcher, ignoring Gemma's protests, and hurried to the crossing point.

I joined them, barely touching Mrs Caro's hand before the world faded away. *Don't worry, Gem*, I thought as the world reformed around us. *Aphros and I will do that every week if that's what it takes. You're going to be just fine.*

7

THE BELL WENT for recess, and blearily I packed up my things and stood. Mum had offered to call me in sick for the day, but there was one certain person I needed to see; I had questions that needed answering.

Sadly, this Tuesday started with drama then health, neither of which I shared with Scott. Still, I'd survived them both and now I had recess to track him down—and find a way to make him talk.

We'd gone back to my house last night and before Mrs Caro had loaded Gemma in the car and taken her home, I'd explained to them all what Aphros and I had done.

Mum asked if Gem would be allowed back in Sanctuary now, but Mrs Caro had shaken her head sadly. "I've had dealings with the Keeper before," she'd said. "She never changes her mind."

"But what if Gemma is healed?" I'd asked.

Mrs Caro had shrugged. "Possibly. But we don't even know if that's possible, Edge. It's not like we've had the opportunity to really study the Valley or its connection to people before. We have no idea what's normal and what's not, and what of it might be reversible."

My stomach had twisted. Actually, we had a perfect way to figure out what was normal and what wasn't, and he would be showing up to school in only a few hours' time.

So here I was, half asleep and yawning my head off as I shoved my books into my locker and retrieved an apple, heading off to find the one person I wanted least in the world to speak to.

I found him on one of the school lawns, surrounded by his stupid mates, laughing with them at something.

I blushed awkwardly, even though I knew it wasn't likely they were laughing at me. "Scott?" I interrupted. "Can I talk to you for a sec?"

Valiantly, I ignored the ooo's and wolf whistling and headed to an empty corner of grass. I stood there with my arms folded protectively over my ribs and watched as Scott extricated himself from his circle of minions. The sly smile slipped off his face as soon as his back turned on them, deepening to something just shy of a frown, eyebrows deeply furrowed.

"Come on," he muttered as he stalked past.

I stayed where I was, not wanting to be seen following his orders—then sighed explosively. I wanted to talk in view of his mates even less.

I followed him around the corner and through a walkway to within sight of the front carpark.

"What?" he said, turning and halting abruptly.

I exhaled my frustration. "How much do you know about what's going on with Gemma?"

He shrugged. "What, you mean the weird fit thing in class yesterday? And the fact that she looks more zombie than human?"

"Yeah. That."

He shrugged again. "What about it?"

I chewed my tongue a little. No matter how I said it, he was going to ark up. "What was it like?" I said. "When you first connected to Valley?"

Immediately, he shot me a suspicious look. "I don't remember. Why?"

I plucked a leaf from a nearby tree, running it through my fingers over and over. "How much do you remember about Gemma's involvement when we... You know." Too many questions. But surely he must know, or have guessed.

His eyes narrowed. "What are you not saying? You think Gemma got contaminated when she tried to help you get me out of the Valley and you think I know how to fix it, is that it? Because I don't, and I had nothing to do with it."

I worked to keep my voice level. "I'm not blaming you for anything, Scott," I said, a hint of bite creeping in despite myself. "No one is."

"Then what do you want?"

I shredded the leaf into tiny pieces and scattered them on the ground like confetti. "Look, no one's accusing you of anything," I said, "because it has nothing to do with you. Gemma's connected to the Valley. Not because you contaminated her," I added firmly as he began to protest, "but because she met the pillar of light and accepted its offer."

Scott paled. His eyes widened for a fraction of a second before he re-exerted control.

I squinted at him. "What's going to happen to her, Scott?"

"I... I have no idea." He leaned away, suddenly transfixed by the traffic outside the school fence.

I closed my eyes, shoulders slumping. "Scott, please. Her connection to the Valley is getting stronger literally every hour. I can see it, and it's terrifying. Even you—" I swallowed, my throat abruptly dry. I stretched my fingers out by my sides. "Even you didn't progress that fast until nearly the end," I said roughly.

Out on the road, a car backfired. Scott jerked, staring at where it had been.

"Do you have any idea why the Valley's hold on Gemma is getting so much stronger so fast?" I asked. "Or why she's going practically catatonic?"

"No," he said curtly.

"Is there anything she can do? Any way to fight it?" *Please, let there be something.*

"No!" Scott faced me at last, hands fisted by his sides. "I told you, I don't know anything, okay? It's not my fault she got caught up with the stupid Valley and I don't know anything that will help! It's not my fault," he repeated. Before I could note that I'd already agreed to that, he continued. "I'm not even connected to the Valley anymore. Check. I know you can." His gaze pinned me, defiant.

I bit my lip. I could, though I had no idea how he knew it. He'd probably guessed I had some sort of funky powers going on, considering I'd literally saved him from darkness that ate your soul, but he didn't know that I was a Road Master—if he even knew what a Road Master was.

It was probably a good idea to make sure the Valley wasn't sinking its claws into Scott again. But even without the Valley, Scott's soulprint was... uncomfortable. It gave me the heebie jeebies every time I brushed against it.

But I needed his help, and if he wouldn't give that, I still needed all the information I could get. I exhaled. "Hold still."

His eyes widened briefly, but he obeyed.

Clenching my teeth, I forced myself to search for his soulprint. I scrunched my eyes shut harder: his soulprint wasn't there.

Eyes still closed, I reached out for him. I brushed his shoulder and the crisp cotton of his uniform shirt. I shifted upward, over his collar to where I could press the tips of my fingers lightly against the skin of his neck. Ah. There was his soulprint, just as usual: a dark night sky, a cold wind, a black hilltop under the stars with a clawing sense of space, vastness... Emptiness.

I pulled away hurriedly, choking down instinctual fear borne both from the actual physical sensations of Scott's soulprint, and the horrible, tangled memories it conjured: Scott, his soulprint ripped and torn, enmeshed in the Valley's grip; another girl, Georgia, face crusted with blood and eyes staring blankly at the roof of the bathroom where I'd found her. I breathed deeply through my nose and focussed on expelling the negative energy, just like the police psychologist had taught me.

I realised Scott was staring at me and turned toward him. "What?" I glanced to where his fingers touched his neck, right where my fingers had been, and a thrill of nerves ran through me. Before all the kerfuffle with the Valley, Scott had harboured a pretty intense crush on me; he'd tried to get my attention every way he'd known how. Pity that ninety-nine percent of them had involved humiliating me.

He'd pretty much ignored me since the Valley incident, so I'd sort of forgotten about it. But now...

I pulled my gaze back to his face, forcing myself to act nonchalant. Now I'd probably better not forget about it again.

"What did you do?"

I ignored his question and regathered my thoughts. "You're not connected to the Valley," I said. "But something is definitely wrong."

His soulprint had been faint, hard to find—but was that because of what was happening *now* in the Valley? Or was it because of his connection a couple of weeks ago? I hadn't exactly been seeking him out to check on his recovery, after all.

"Take me with you."

I blinked at him. "Sorry, what?"

"Take me with you." His gaze was unflinching as he clenched his hands.

"*Where?*"

"You know where."

"Actually, I—" I stopped.

There was really only one place he could be referring to, wasn't there? "*Sanctuary?*" I asked, voice pitched low.

He nodded, a short, jerky movement that looked like it cost him far more than it should have. "Sanctuary."

My eyebrows creased together. "But—can't you just go yourself?"

His jaw worked. "No. My mum—I only—I don't know how."

There was a whole lot of information to be mined in that broken whale of a sentence, if only I had the time and brainpower. But Scott, being almost literally the root of all evil for a time there—well, it had never occurred to me that he might not know how to get into the better parts of the other world.

"I'll... consider it?" Voluntarily taking Scott to Sanctuary? It seemed a little like inviting the fox into your chicken coop, and I wasn't quite sure how I felt about it.

Scott's jaw worked again, and I wasn't sure if he was preparing to argue with me or what. "I'll help you," he blurted.

The half-time bell rang. "What?"

"Take me with you. Show me how to get there, to... You know. Show me, and I'll tell you what I know about..." He swallowed. "About what's wrong with Gemma."

I stared as students streamed around us, laughing and chatting and shouting in the middle of their carefree lunchbreak. A quiet breeze lifted wisps of hair off my face. "Promise?"

Scott's hands clenched again as he nodded. "I'll tell you," he said. "I promise."

8

I ARRIVED IN the glade after school, half expecting Scott not to be there. But he was ready and waiting, pacing back and forth and trying just a little too hard not to look at the crossing to the Valley on the other side of the tea-coloured creek.

"You okay?" I said as I sat on a rock. At my feet, a host of out-of-place plants grew—feathery carrot tops, their roots nearly ready for picking; a small host of native paper daisies; and a little way behind, a neat row of sunflowers, merrily bobbing their heads in the hot afternoon sunshine.

Scott stopped short. "Yeah. Fine."

And my name was Googlymuffin, and Gemma was in perfect health. Yup. Just fine. I motioned him to a nearby rock. Once he'd perched gingerly on the edge of it, shoulders tight, I pulled a packet of seeds from my pocket and flashed it at him.

His eyebrows lifted. "Carrots?" he said. "I thought you were showing me how to get to Sanctuary, not... *gardening*." He waved dismissively at the plants.

Okay, now I did roll my eyes. "Less sass, more listening," I commanded. I shook a couple of tiny carrot seeds onto my palm and held them out. "Step one, seeds." I glanced up to see him concentrating on my hand. "You used death sacrifices to power your crossing to the Valley. We use life magic, contained in seeds."

His jaw worked. "You used shadow magic too."

I snatched my hand back, fingers closing protectively around the seeds. "Yeah, but I never killed anything to do it."

Scott frowned. "Then how did you do it?"

"I sacrificed part of myself, okay?" I snapped. Memories of my hand sliced open, blood dripping to the ground to power the crossing...

Nausea welled in my stomach, just as it had after using the death magic.

I hadn't turned into a monster as I'd feared, and it had been totally necessary at the time, given Scott had been almost completely possessed by the Valley and only a few minutes away from taking over the world—but it wasn't something I enjoyed thinking about. Not least because it had hurt like someone pulling my brain out my nose with a hot poker. "I thought you were here to learn about life magic."

Scott held his hands up with his palms facing me. "Whoa, I am. Sorry!"

I glared at him for a moment longer, then held out the seeds again. "Look, the principle's exactly the same," I said. "Visualise where you want to go, shove the seed in the soil, and use your travelling abilities to activate the life magic in the seed."

Scott tilted his head. "The life of the seed powers the crossing?"

"That is literally what I just said."

"So why doesn't the seed die? I mean, you're using its life to power your crossing, so how does it still have life left?"

I snapped my mouth closed and glared at him some more. "Because life creates more life." That seemed plausible, right? Mentally I added his question to a growing list of things to ask Quoise.

He shook his head. "That doesn't make sense. If—"

"Look, it just works, okay? Are we going to do this or not? Because I totally have other things I could be doing..." I licked the tip of one finger and stuck a carrot seed on it.

Scott held his hands up again. "I hope you're not going to be a teacher when you grow up."

I narrowed my eyes and stretched a deliberately fake smile into place, tucking the seed packet back into my pocket. "Give me your hand."

He blinked. "My hand? Why?"

I hissed through my teeth. "So I can transport you to Sanctuary, idiot. Hand?"

He stretched out hesitantly and took my free hand. His palm was warm and soft—but the skin contact heightened my road mastery. I tightened my grip so I wouldn't accidentally pull away in response to the cold, prickling emptiness of his soulprint.

Scott stared intently at our joined hands.

Quickly, I shoved my finger with the seed on it into the ground and made the crossing to Sanctuary.

The instant we arrived, I bounced to my feet, releasing Scott and dusting myself off.

I stalked to the far side of the entrance alcove, where the rockery tumbled and swirled, grey boulders the size of wombats spiralling across a field of white pebbles.

Scott followed. I tried not to watch him, but from the corner of my eye I could see him staring openly at his new surroundings, and part of me was deathly curious: what would he think of Sanctuary?

"It's so quiet," he said softly as he stopped next to me, still peering around. "It's..." He drew in a long, steadying breath.

"Yeah," I said. "Calming hormones. I have no clue how it does it, but being here increases your body's production of calming hormones. Here," I added. "Watch this."

Amidst the rockery, small, red-leafed bushes glimmered and flickered like fire. I plucked a leaf off one and crouched where two of the larger grey rocks met and formed a crevice—a cave for something small. It seemed a likely spot. I waggled the leaf enticingly. *Come on. Come out and play.*

Ah ha. Deep in the shadow, something moved. Behind me, Scott started to speak, but I waved at him urgently with my free hand, and he quietened.

Waggle waggle. *Heeeeere, little critter. Come get the leaf. Nice, tasty, flaming leaf...*

Pounce! One instant, just a leaf: the next, a fire-bright lizard-shaped creature hung from it, large, hinged jaws snapped tight on the leathery frond. I swung it around and dangled it at Scott.

He eyed it suspiciously. "What is it?"

"Fire salamander." I offered it to him. "Go on. Take it."

Cautiously, he reached out toward the foot-long lizard. An inch away, he stopped. "Will it bite?"

I smiled a gentle baby-panda of a smile. "Trust me."

For just a second he flicked his gaze toward me and his eyes met mine. "I do."

He took the lizard more carefully than I'd have expected, but his grip was sure and gentle, like he was used to handling animals. My stomach dropped as I remembered a tiny white mouse, near dead, right before Scott had wrung its neck.

Scott laughed—not at me, but a tiny, barely-heard sound of genuine delight. The salamander was licking his thumb while warm, happy flames radiated from its back.

Oh. That was... unexpected. Maybe he wasn't a complete monster after all. "Come on," I said. "I'll show you the unicorns."

He followed, still cradling the salamander as we left the entrance alcove.

Halfway to the stables, I realised that a small flock of fairies was making their way down from the Lodge, and that they would reach the stables at about the same time we would. I licked my lower lip, wondering how they would take to Scott.

Scott had noticed them too, casting nervous glances at them as we continued up the hillside.

Even though Sanctuary lived in perpetual twilight, it felt darker than usual this afternoon. Or maybe that was just the lack of Gemma; nearing the stables with Scott by my side instead felt a little surreal.

Aphros appeared in the doorway of the stables, and abruptly, some of Scott's tension melted.

I'd forgotten that they'd met while Aphros was trapped in the Valley. Though, had I remembered, I certainly wouldn't have expected a welcome this affectionate—from either of them.

I hesitated a few paces away. Maybe this was why Scott had wanted to visit Sanctuary so much?

They seemed pretty darn friendly. Especially considering that I was the one who'd saved Aphros from the clutches of the Valley's evil soulprint—the evil soulprint Scott had brought to life.

A tiny, logical part of me that I didn't want to listen to right now pointed out that I could literally speak straight to Aphros's mind; Scott was hardly going to replace me.

And then I didn't have the chance to listen to any part of me, logical or not, because the fairies arrived, the Keeper at the front in her emerald-green tunic and tiny gold coronet.

"What are you doing?" she hissed—at Scott, at Aphros, or maybe both?

Aphros turned to her. "Welcoming a newcomer," she said mildly.

In the depths of the stables, the twin baby unicorns whinnied.

"*Newcomer*? Fraternising with the enemy, more like," the Keeper replied, planting her hands on her hips.

Aphros tossed her mane, the point of her horn scribing an arc dangerously close to a gold-winged fairy. "That is a matter of history," she said, stamping a hoof. "I make friends in the present."

"And I'm sure that works out very well for you," the Keeper said, "but it is my job to keep the trad-itions of Sanctuary, and I'm quite attached to history." She shifted her gaze to Scott, who caught her eye briefly before staring off toward the pines that separated the meadow from the beach.

"As for you," the Keeper continued, her voice heavy with distaste, "I cannot even understand why you would show your face here, after all you did, and nearly did. Are you that proud, that you must come in here to gloat?"

Scott didn't reply, though his fingers twitched by his sides.

"I brought him here," I said, stepping forward.

"Yes, I should have guessed as much," the Keeper replied with a similar level of disgust. "Queen Rule Breaker herself."

My stomach did a complicated flip-flop. "I only break rules," I said through clenched teeth, reminding myself of all the reasons I couldn't— shouldn't—shout at the ruler of the fairies, "when someone's life is at stake."

The Keeper's left eyebrow didn't believe me. "Oh? And whose life is at stake, that you would bring him"—she jabbed the word at Scott—"here?"

"I didn't know bringing him here was against the rules," I shot back. "It seems like they're changing daily." I inhaled sharply, hoping I hadn't just crossed an irreversible line.

The Keeper pursed her lips. "Well. I suppose you'll just have to learn to keep up, won't you." She gave me a saccharine smile and turned to Scott. "Scott Anthony Harden, you are herewith formally banned from Sanctuary. If I catch you here again, you can be sure it will end unpleasantly."

"Oh, because today's visit was such a picnic." I glared at her.

She glanced disinterestedly at me. "Be careful, Emma Louise Tanning. You are on your last warning yourself." With that parting blow, she led her posse of fairies back up the hill.

"Lovely creature," said Scott. "Is she always so friendly?"

Aphros snorted.

I shook my head. "Come on. We'd better go."

"Why?" Scott said, eyebrows lifting in mild surprise. "She's gone."

I shook my head again. "The fairies can sense it if we stay here. They're all... They can sense who's in Sanctuary," I added, not wanting to get into the fine details of road mastery right now.

He nodded, expressionless. "So let's go, I guess."

We farewelled Aphros and set off back toward the entrance alcove.

"What else have *you* done to piss her off?"

I cut him a sharp glance, but he seemed to be asking genuinely enough. "Apart from illegally entering the Valley to get rid of the shadows and save your life? Brought Gemma here for help."

His eyebrows were even more surprised this time, and he walked backward for a few steps, watching my face. "You're kidding."

"Nope. They kicked her out and told her never to come back, same as you."

Scott stuck his hands deep into his pockets. "Friendly bunch. I can see why this is supposed to be the land of all that's good and pure."

I glared at him—but a weightier thought intruded. "You'll still tell me, though?" I said. "What you know about Gem? Even though the Keeper kicked you out?" In my defence, I'd had no idea the Keeper would react like that, although I supposed a less-than-rosy greeting should have been expected. But... "It wasn't like it was Gem's fault," I added quietly.

He shrugged, hands still in his pockets, and tears of anger welled in my eyes. "Hey," he said sharply as they spilled over onto my cheeks. "None of that. Of course I'll still tell you."

I inhaled, swiping at my cheeks. "I'm not crying," I said. "I'm angry."

"Yeah, my eyes leak all the time when I'm mad, too."

"Shut up."

We entered the alcove and I exhaled noisily. "No. Don't shut up. Talk. Tell me what you know."

Scott nodded. "I will. Promise." He hesitated, side-eyeing me. "Tomorrow."

"Tomorrow? Gemma could be dead by then!"

He drew back, alarmed. "No way. It doesn't happen that fast."

I shrugged. "It pretty much is this time."

Scott puffed up his cheeks and released his breath slowly. "I guess it makes sense. You didn't actually damage the Valley at all, you know. You just... disconnected it from its current body."

"*Your* body." Oh, oops. Probably shouldn't have reminded him of that.

Reminded. Ha. As if he'd ever be able to forget.

"My body," he agreed carefully. "And whatever... *humanity* it had managed to absorb. But you didn't fundamentally change it, or distil any of its power, and now it has a new human connection—and this time it knows exactly what it's doing."

"Help me," I said levelly, trying to pin him with my gaze. "Help me fight it."

He shook his head, not a negative, just... overwhelmed, I realised. "You have no idea what you're asking."

"So tell me."

He met my gaze briefly. "I will," he said. "Tomorrow."

"I said, tomorrow she could—"

He cut me off with a wave. "There's something you need to see first, to understand. I'll bring it to school. Tomorrow." He said it firmly, and I knew this time there'd be no arguing.

Stubborn git-face. "Fine," I said, because what other choice did I have? "Tomorrow. First thing. I'll meet you at my locker. *First thing.*"

He nodded and stretched out a hand. "First thing."

I stared at his hand. Did he want me to shake it? Because he wasn't holding it right if he was.

Sensing my confusion, Scott gestured impatiently. "To go back?"

Oh. Right. Of course.

I took his hand. "It might be late when we get back," I warned. "The time slips happen at random without a fairy to help."

He bared his teeth, and if I didn't look too closely, it might have been a smile. "That's fine," he said. "No one at my house cares what I do."

I sat on the grass and closed my eyes. "Well, here's hoping it's not too wildly out," I said. "Because at my house, everyone cares what I do."

9

THE BELL WENT for lunch and I slammed my science textbook shut.

I'd waited by my locker until the last possible moment both before school and at recess—still no Scott. I'd sat through a double period of Maths, then a lesson of English, and now Science—all classes I shared with both Gemma and Scott—but there'd been no Scott. My chances of him showing up for the day now were slim to none.

I fought my way out of the classroom a little more vigorously than usual, and once I had finally reached my locker and shoved my books inside, I slammed the door shut viciously. This would teach me to trust evil, shadow-spawning, good-for-nothing morons with pretty hair.

Really, the pretty hair should have been the giveaway, I thought as I snatched my sandwich out of my bag. Showed he was really just a selfish idiot who only cared about appearances.

A sea of students ebbed and flowed around me, and I cast about for direction, oddly adrift. There was no Gemma to follow, no Scott to avoid.

I clenched my free hand—and then, just for the feel of it, pinched my sandwich until my thumb and forefinger met through the bread. Untrustworthy froghead.

I stomped across the lawns and found an unoccupied bit of garden edging to perch on. I could only hope that the block Aphros and I had done would hold.

If not, I'd sneak Gemma in again and we'd do another one. Again, and again, and again, until I figured out a way to fix this, if that's what it took.

Something thumped onto the paved path at my feet. I blinked, then craned up to see who'd dumped the book.

My heart practically clawed at my ribcage. Standing with his back to the sun so it glowed around him like a misplaced halo—was Scott.

"What the—"

He shifted, halo diminishing—and I could see how complicated his face looked, eyes sad and scared, lips tight to match the line of his shoulders. "Just read it," he said.

"But what is it?" I glanced back at the thick, worn book—journal?—lying on the ground.

"Nothing," he said. "Just read it." He twitched, fingers curling as though he wanted to reach down and grab it. A moment of pain and longing, then he stalked away.

"Hey!" I called, standing. He ignored me, and what else could I say? Come back? I need your help? Where have you been all morning? Why weren't you here when I needed you?

I swallowed hard and screwed my eyes shut against welling tears. None of that. I couldn't say any of it, not to Scott, not here.

A cloud crossed over the sun and the world dimmed to muted greys. I picked up the book, sat back down, and let it fall open on my lap.

It settled somewhere about three quarters of the way through, revealing page after page of careful, deliberate handwriting. Scott's?

January 12. Nothing new.

January 13. Nothing important.

January 14. Nothing that matters.

I turned to the front, wondering if there would be an explanation. Was this some kind of weird diary after all? Scott definitely didn't strike me as the kind of person who'd keep a diary, but then again, you never knew.

The front page was blank, but the second page... I frowned.

I am Scott Anthony Harden. My birthday is July 9. If I am in trouble, I should call 000 and ask for the police.

The next lines listed his address and a note that he lived with his Mum and Dad—but it had all been crossed out, with a line ruled neatly through it.

'With Mum' had an extra line—probably, I realised, squinting at it closely, because it had been crossed out first, before the rest of the sentence.

Below, written neatly, was 'I live with Aunt Sally', with a slightly more distant address.

I traced a finger over the ruled-out lines, chest constricting, brow knitting. He'd moved, no longer with his parents but an aunt—and his mum had somehow gone first.

I turned the page.

Mum is five foot six with dark hair and dark eyes. She gets angry easily, especially when she comes home late at night—avoid morning after. I frowned. Why would Scott want me to know this? How did it help? And why not just tell me, rather than writing it down?

Spare money usually in sock drawer—the top right one—socks are for feet (warmth). Pizza (good food) delivery is 120 000. Press those numbers into the spare phone Dad gave you—hidden under the loose floorboard at the foot of my bed (sleeping place). Do not call Dad.

Abruptly, I flicked the page over. These notes seemed far too personal; surely Scott hadn't intended for me to read that part.

I cleared my throat, letting the journal rest open on my lap as I scrubbed my sweaty palms against my thighs.

The next page wasn't any better, beginning, "Dad is usually out of town working." Hurriedly, I skipped to the end.

Blank. I flipped back until I found Scott's writing again, then turned back a small chunk of pages.

November 27. I forgot my name today. It's been months since I've forgotten anything—the gaps seem to actually be healing now, and I haven't forgotten anything since I... Since Mum left. But I forgot my name today, and I didn't have the book to remind me, and I panicked.

Then the new girl, Emma, asked me—Scott, right?— and all I could do was nod.

She didn't care, just sat down next to me, half ignoring me as she explained that the teacher had told her to work with me this lesson—and we did, we worked, and she never said much and I never had to worry about whether she'd ask me something I couldn't answer, and I didn't care if my name was Scott or Steve, because who I was didn't matter to her, and I could have been anyone.

A couple of blank lines, and then in a different coloured pen, an annotation:

I never want to be Someone again.

November 27. That would have been my first week at the school, at the end of last year when we'd moved up suddenly from Melbourne. I'd forgotten I'd ever worked with Scott on anything. That had been... in English, maybe?

I glanced back to where he'd written my name, and adrenalin spiked through my stomach. I remembered speculating at one point that all I'd done for Scott to be infatuated with me was ignore him, not falling over myself at him like everyone else. Scary how true my throwaway comment seemed to have been.

But how did this help me with Gem?

Wait, he'd said something about forgetting.

Lightning struck in my head, and I clenched the book.

Memories. Scott had been losing his memories, and this was where he'd recorded everything he'd need to know if he suddenly forgot something important.

The Valley. The Valley must have made him lose his memories—at least in the beginning, because he'd said in that entry about me (nerves ran through me again) that he hadn't forgotten anything for a while.

Gem didn't seem to be forgetting anything. Was that because it was all happening too fast? Surely that would have sped up the memory loss too—unless the Valley had all the memories it needed?

I flipped back to near the start of the book and began hunting for anything that sounded magical, anything that might be linked to the Valley—or death magic.

My stomach churned and despite the heat of the day, goosebumps rose on my arms; what if memory loss was the result of using death magic?

I couldn't *think* of anything I'd forgotten; there didn't *seem* to be any holes in my memories—but if I'd forgotten, if using death magic had stolen things from me, would I even know before it was too late? Suddenly, Scott's obsessive annotating—'socks are for feet (warmth)'—made sense.

But this line of thought wasn't helping Gem. I shook my head and resumed skimming the entries in the journal.

Gradually, over the next half hour, a picture formed: Scott (and possibly his mother?) had travelled on something he only called 'the roads' to find the heart of the Valley, a physical location that it seemed could only be reached on said roads—and there, something had happened. He avoided saying it outright, and I guessed it was one memory he wouldn't be sorry to lose. But whatever else had happened, the Valley had been woken there.

The warning bell for the end of lunch rang, and I stood, hugging the journal to my chest, lighter than I'd been in days. The power of the Valley had a physical location, and it could be woken—which meant it could be put back to sleep. If I could find this place, put the Valley back to sleep...

Surely then the connection between Gem and the Valley would disappear, and she would be okay. Surely that kind of disconnection wouldn't harm her, because I wouldn't be messing around with her soulprint; the connection would just... vanish.

I hugged the journal again and tucked it carefully into my locker—Scott seemed to have totally disappeared once more.

That was a pain—I had approximately a thousand million questions to ask him now—but at least—at *least*—I had a plan.

Find roads.

Find Valley's power.

Shut it down.

Save Gemma.

Lists. Lists really did make the world seem bright.

10

I DIDN'T MANAGE to find Scott again for the rest of the day, so as soon as I got home, I changed out of my uniform and ran down to the glade. If I couldn't ask Scott about the roads, at least I could brainstorm with Aphros.

I arrived in Sanctuary and sought out Aphros, not with my road mastery, but with our mysterious connection that had developed when Aphros had joined her soulprint with mine in our final battle against the Valley.

A hint of minty freshness drifted through the air and instinctively I breathed deeply. Aphros's soft green-and-gold soulprint blossomed against my senses, a trail of colour and scent winding through the grass at my feet.

Aphros's soulprint led me out of the alcove, up the meadow, past the Lodge, and to a small garden of trees and pale-coloured flowers. As I neared, the trail broadened, becoming brighter and clearer to my senses—and it was joined by another pair of trails, also pale green and gold, but one with a hint of cornflower blue and the other with twirls of bronze. My lips twitched upward. The unicorn babies always brought a smile.

"Hi, Aphros," I said as I approached her. She stood with her back to me, watching the two foals frolicking in the grass. Lily, the one with the blue in her soulprint, sniffed at a bush covered in the little white star flowers that were everywhere in Sanctuary, and sneezed. Filibere, the bronze twin, flared his nostrils at me warily. "It's just me," I told him, holding out my hand. He cautiously inched closer, propped about two paces away, and dashed around the clearing before coming to a halt behind his mother.

I gave him half a smile. "Yeah. I'd hide too if I thought it'd do any good."

"Wouldn't we all," a soft voice muttered— Quoise, appearing from behind a tree.

"Hi," I told her, and she greeted me back. "So, I have news," I said, plopping down on the ground beside Aphros.

Quoise fluttered down to perch nearby. "Oh? How's Gem?"

"Did the block hold?" Aphros added, nose twitching.

I nodded. "I think so. I haven't seen her today yet though. But Mrs Caro would have called if something had gone wrong, I'm sure of it." She'd helped me get out of school once before to save Gem; I knew she wouldn't hesitate to do it again if Gemma really needed me. "But I talked to Scott today."

Quoise leaned closer; Aphros's ears twitched.

"Well. Talked, not so much. He showed me a journal," I amended. My pulse jumped and I licked my lips. "Did you know he was losing his memories?" I said, turning to Aphros.

She shook her mane. "No. He showed no signs of this while I knew him."

I puffed my cheeks up and exhaled. "It had probably stopped by then. It seems," I said carefully, "like the memory loss was connected to something he called the roads. And on these roads is a physical location where we can access the power of the Valley."

Quoise stiffened immediately, and Aphros stomped her hint foot.

"What?" I said as Quoise looked back at Aphros, eyes wide like she was pleading. I looked back and forth between the two of them, then planted my fists on my hips. "Alright, what's going on? What are you two not saying?"

They held their gaze a while longer, and I opened my mouth, but Quoise sighed, shoulders slumping, and turned toward me. "A lot," she muttered, with a furious glance at Aphros. "There's a lot we're not saying."

Aphros snorted. "You can say that again."

"Wow, thank you. That's so helpful."

Quoise sighed. "You tell her," she said, nodding to Aphros.

Aphros shook out her mane. "It's your mess," she muttered, but she swung toward me. "I'm not sure where to start, exactly," she said. "As far as I know"—she shot a hard glare at Quoise—"Sanctuary and the Valley were both created in the same way."

Quoise shrugged. "That's what I've always been told."

"Wait," I interjected. "Sanctuary and the Valley were *created*? By who?"

Quoise shrugged again. "I'm not sure if the Keeper knows and isn't saying, or is just pretending she knows so she can lord it over the rest of us." She gasped, hands flying up to cover her mouth. "I can't believe I said that," she mumbled through her fingers, eyes wide.

Aphros snorted again. "This is your influence on her you know," she said to me.

I opened my mouth to protest but caught a glimmer in her eye. I grinned instead. "Okay, so the Valley and Sanctuary were created in the same way. How does that relate to Gem?"

"You are familiar with the balance," Aphros said, and I nodded.

"That was the representation of Sanctuary and the Valley's magics. It isn't real, it is a projection, but the *sources* of the magics? Those are real."

I frowned. "So Scott's right. Somewhere out there"—I gestured broadly—"is not only a magic box that powers the Valley, but also one that powers Sanctuary."

Aphros exchanged a glance with Quoise. "Essentially, yes. You got close to the Valley's power source when you entered the sinkhole to find Gemma—and Scott."

I nodded. "From what I can see, Scott's suggesting that we find the Valley's power source on these roads, then we might be able to shut it down. That wouldn't damage Gem like trying to actually remove the connection, would it?"

Aphros tilted her head. "I *think* not."

Quoise buzzed her wings in agitation. "For the record, I think this is a very bad idea. Going anywhere near the Valley is dangerous, let alone into the very source of power itself."

"I survived the sinkhole last time," I pointed out.

Aphros cleared her throat.

"Well, yes, with help."

Quoise shook her head. "Don't underestimate this, Edge. You made it out. But a fairy died last time, remember?"

My stomach flopped. "I remember."

"That's part of why the Keeper is so scared of Gem being here," Quoise continued. "Sanctuary's magic is literally all that keeps us alive. Earth has a little magic, enough that we can travel over for visits, but the Valley—the Valley has nothing to sustain us, so if we cross over there, we die. Instantly. And Gemma being here... It's like she's bringing the Valley's magic into Sanctuary. For us, that could literally be life threatening."

I folded my arms across my chest. "You didn't seem to be too threatened when the Valley's shadows were trying to *take over* Sanctuary earlier in the year."

"Don't assume you know everything that goes on in the Lodge," Quoise said evenly. "Just because we didn't project panic doesn't mean people weren't worried. Why do you think I helped you?"

I shook my head. This *did* explain why Quoise had seemed so reluctant to help me, and why she'd given me the unicorn-hair ward without really telling me what to do with it. "Okay," I said. "I acknowledge that this is a really dangerous thing to do. But do you have any better suggestions for how to fix Gemma? Any other secrets that might help?"

She sniffed softly. "Plenty of secrets. None that may help, other than your hair-brained scheme."

"*Scott's* hair-brained scheme," I pointed out.

"Strangely enough, that's not encouraging."

Aphros snorted. "Maybe you could take a walk down to the Lodge," she murmured.

I glanced sharply at her. "Why the Lodge? I thought we weren't talking to the fairies about this. Quoise excepted, obviously."

"Library?" Aphros said over my head at Quoise.

Quoise's wings snapped out and she shot a metre up into the air. "Yes. If we have any information on these roads, that's where it'll be." She grinned. "So, Edge, breaker of all the fairies' rules, how would you feel about a little trespassing?"

"Will it help Gemma?" I asked, standing up.

"Probably," Quoise said, "though I can't promise."

"I'm in," I said. "Like you even had to ask."

She led the way from the garden as the twin unicorns collapsed in an adorable heap by Aphros, exhausted from their exploring.

My heart hammered. We had a plan, and we were doing something about it. "Just a little bit longer," I murmured, thinking of Gem. "Hold on."

11

QUOISE HAD LED me through winding corridors in the Lodge until at last she'd stopped in front of a dark wooden door. She'd opened it with a flourish. "Ta da!"

I'd peeked through, and my jaw had dropped. Shelves rose far above my head, at least two storeys high—and where they ended the room kept going, a vast void at least another two storeys high, dotted with the same kinds of fairy furniture I'd seen in the main foyer: small tables and chairs sprouting from the walls, comfy couches, hammocks and cushions suspended from the roof at different heights, a few platforms rising out of the shelves themselves.

And all around, the walls were utterly filled with books, all the way to the magnificent roof, where intricate floral and leafy patterns twisted and wound, making the ceiling seem like a living garden. I could live in this cavernous room for the rest of my life.

"Pretty, isn't it?" Quoise had said as I'd stepped, awed, into the space.

"Uh huh."

"We don't generally let visitors in here, you know. Come on. Keep your head down and look innocent." She had let the wooden door fall shut behind us. "For this we need the restricted section."

And now we'd been in the restricted section for nearly an hour, hunkering down behind shelves every time someone came close. The tiny text of the book in my lap was blurring, and my stomach rumbled. I slammed the fairy-sized book closed—inasmuch as it was possible to slam a book the size of my phone—and leaned back against the shelves.

"Nothing?" said Quoise. Her voice sounded flat and tired.

"Not a thing," I said.

"I'm so sorry," Quoise said. "I was so sure there would be something here. We write *everything* down. I must not have the search terms right." She dragged a hand over her face.

"It's fine," I said, closing my eyes as I leaned against a shelf. "We'll find something eventually."

Quoise kicked the shelf she hovered next to, the movement jolting her in the air. "It's just so stupid," she said. "Before I met you, I never questioned any of this." She gestured broadly at the library around us. "But last month, with the shadows, and Aphros, and *you*..." She shook her head.

"What *about* me, though?" I said, propping one elbow on the shelf and leaning my head on my hand. "What can I do that you guys can't? You said that things were happening here in the Lodge to deal with the shadows, but it sure didn't look like it. You're all Road Masters," I pointed out. "So what did I do that you couldn't have done?"

Quoise sighed, a full-bodied exhale that left her sagging, defeated. "You're a Road Master, Edge," she said tiredly.

My brows crinkled. "I know that."

"But you don't know what it *means*," she said, staring at the books on the shelf. "Because I didn't tell you. I'm not supposed to."

I sat very still.

"You can do a lot more than you think," she said at last. "We can sense everyone's soulprints. But unlike you, we can't manipulate them. What you did, separating Scott's soulprint from the Valley? We can't do anything direct like that. We can see, but not touch."

"I can only do that with Aphros's help, though," I said.

"For now."

The room didn't move, but it might as well have. "So you're *not* Road Masters?"

Quoise shrugged. "To-may-to, to-mah-to."

"So what else can I do that you can't?"

She frowned. "Hold on, road mastery. That's it!" She shot up into the air and disappeared.

I sat, wondering if I was supposed to follow her.

I didn't have to wait long; she returned shortly, carrying a vivid green book, the exact colour of new spring grass. She dropped it on my lap. Embossed gold lettering curled across the cover, tendrils snaking to the edges and over the spine.

Through Roads Between: a field guide to road mastery.

"Road mastery!" Quoise explained, wings quivering with excitement. "There might not be anything on Scott's roads or the heart of the Valley specifically in the library, but everything there is to know about road mastery is here. Open it!" She gestured at the volume, almost as tall as she was and at least an inch thick.

"How did you even carry this?" I mused as I flipped it open. I skimmed down the contents until my fingers found Chapter Five: On The Roads. That sounded promising.

The chapter header was in the same curling, dangerous font as the cover. I skimmed through a couple of paragraphs, then settled into reading.

Thus far we have explored the various ways to use road mastery skills in the everyday world, the text read. *But the true purpose of road mastery—and indeed, the talent for which it is named—is to enable those equipped with such a skill to travel the Roads Between. These roads extend between the waypoints and the worlds and are usually by-passed by the skill of travelling, or moving instantaneously from one location to another. However, while the traveller is limited to visiting only places that they can clearly envisage in their mind, using the roads enables the road master to explore and discover organically.*

"This sounds promising," I said to Quoise, who perched on the shelf behind me so she could read over my shoulder.

"But does it say anything about what the roads *are*?"

"I dunno." I skimmed a finger further down the page. "This bit sounds right, though."

The Roads Between are dangerous and generally impassable, I read aloud. *Consisting of the chaotic soup from which the likes of the Valley of Sanctuary and Repose was carved. All dangers, all confusion, all chaos exist therein, and for a non-Road Master to step on them alone is death. Road Masters, however, may sense the thread of purpose that unites the roads together, and may follow it from one land to another.* I craned around to Quoise. "Sanctuary was *carved*? By who?" I added when she nodded.

She shrugged. "No idea. That's just what we've always been told. It could just be a story, a myth."

I read on. *There are two things to consider when contemplating the use of the roads: firstly, how to navigate them, and secondly, how to find them. Although this might seem a counter-intuitive order, to find the roads without knowing how to navigate them is as much a trap for the Road Master as for the ordinary person, for a Road Master can find the sensory input of the roads overwhelming unless they have been conditioned and are prepared for what they will experience.*

Indeed, it is a surfeit of sensory input that indicates the location of the roads; a whiff of scent where none should belong, a half-heard noise with no apparent origin; any sensory signs that are over and beyond expectations for that location; these are clear signs that the roads are near.

Quoise stiffened.

"What? What is it?"

Her eyes widened, bright and excited. "I know where the roads are."

"*What?*"

"The roads. Scott's right. There *is* a way to the power source of the Valley, and I know how to find it."

Adrenalin leapt through me and I leaned toward her. "You can get me there?"

She shook her head. "I can't travel on the roads—the book is right," she said, gesturing to where it lay in my lap. "You need a proper Road Master to travel these roads, like you. I can't travel with you," Quoise said, shaking her head, "but I can get you to the entrance. There's a place... You'll get wet. But there's a cave, down by the beach, I think it should be large enough for you to fit. Inside, the air is strange, and every now and then you can hear echoes, like stray soulprints hovering in the air. I've been there a few times, and..."

She shivered and met my eye intently. "Edge, if it's true, if where I'm thinking of is the start of the roads, you can't just wander onto them, not without training. There are massive power blocks in place that you'd have to break through—they're there to stop people wandering in accidentally, but they're strong, and..." She swallowed. "You could... get hurt. And then you'd have to know what you were doing once you were *on* the roads. If this book is right, if it's the place I'm thinking of, you could end up stranded over there, unable to move or think, completely overwhelmed."

"Slow eventual death?" I asked.

She nodded. "Slow eventual death. Please. Just... think about this, before you try it. You need training. Somehow." She rubbed her face, frustration wrinkling her brow.

I shook my head. "I'm doing it. You know I am." I held up a hand to forestall her protests. "But I don't have to do it alone, and I don't need to spend weeks training. If I took someone with me who'd been on the roads before, that would make it okay, right?"

"Maybe, but—"

"Scott," I said levelly, holding her gaze.

Quoise inhaled sharply. Doubt and fear crossed her face, but she drew herself together and they melted into simple concern. She nodded, a short, sharp jerk of acknowledgement. "Yes. That makes sense. If what you've told me about him is true, if he's been on the roads as a non-Road Master... Well, that would explain the memory loss. He's *not* a Road Master—goodness knows how he found the roads," she added, frowning—"so when he travelled the roads, they took some of his memories as payment."

That... made a lot of sense. Except for the bit about him getting onto the roads. Could he be a Road Master without anyone knowing, perhaps? Quoise had only realised I was because I'd told her about the trails I could see. Maybe he was hiding something else after all—maybe that's why he'd wanted me to read the journal, rather than telling me about it face-to-face—he didn't want to risk accidentally telling me too much.

"And provided he hasn't lost any of *those* memories," Quoise continued, "then yes. Yes, that would work."

I nodded decisively and stood, stretching out my neck. "Well then. I guess I'd better go convince him to help me."

"Edge," Quoise said, fluttering up and resting her fingertips on my cheek. "Oh, Edge. Be careful."

"Always," I said, smiling, and we both knew that while it wasn't exactly a lie, there was definitely a large helping of wishful thinking. "I promise."

One day, I'd learn not to make promises I wasn't sure I could keep.

But in the meantime, I had a Scott to convince, and I needed all the bluff I could get.

12

AS I HEADED back down the slope from the Lodge, the smell of salt drifted in from Sanctuary's beach. I peered over at the pine trees that separated meadow from sand. Somewhere over that way lay Gemma's only hope.

A niggling at my road mastery drew my attention to the entrance alcove. I pursed my lips. Scott. *My* only hope—at least if I wanted to stay sane while on the roads. But what on earth was he doing here?

He opened his mouth as I approached, but I shook my head in warning. I grabbed his arm and practically dragged him back to the alcove. "What are you *doing* here?" I said. "The Keeper banned you!"

Scott shrugged, extricating his arm from my grip. "So? I needed to talk to you. Where else was I supposed to find you?"

"Oh, I don't know, at *school*? What happened? I looked everywhere for you!"

He shifted awkwardly. "Sorry. Did you read it?"

Abruptly, I sagged. I had bigger things to worry about than fighting with Scott about—well, anything. And really, Scott had bigger things to worry about too. "Yeah. I read it. I... I'm sorry."

Scott shrugged again. "It happens."

Yeah, losing your memory from magical roads and being possessed by the Valley of Death; no big deal. Happens all the time. "So what did you want to talk to me about?" I stepped a few paces to the left to perch on one of the rockery's better-sized boulders. Better to chat here than back home; here, I had Sanctuary's calming atmosphere on my side, and if we hung out near the entry we could easily escape in time if the fairies noticed Scott's presence.

(How they could miss him at all was the real mystery; here in Sanctuary, his soulprint was back to full strength again, and the sense of vastness tugged constantly at the edge of my awareness. He wasn't connected to the Valley anymore, but there was *some*thing going on with his soulprint, that was certain.)

Scott said nothing.

I ground my teeth. I couldn't press him too hard; I really did need his help. But how could I convince him to talk?

Anna.

My sister was an expert at getting information out of people, whether they wanted to talk or not. What would she do in this situation?

Ha, right. Reverse psychology it was.

"It's okay," I said. "If you can't talk about it. I found some information in the library about the roads that might help."

He shot me a wary glance, full of suspicion. "What information?"

My turn to shrug. "I'm a Road Master. That's how I saved you, back... you know. Anyway, I'm a Road Master, which means I can sense people's, uh, soulprints. Auras, sort of. Quoise found a book in their library that explain how Road Masters can use the roads you mentioned."

He stared at me intently. "I know what the books say. The books are wrong."

I didn't hit him in the face, and I mentally awarded myself five million points for restraint. "Look," I said. "The heart of the Valley is on the roads. Gemma is connected to the Valley. If I go on these roads, I can get to the Valley, shut it back down again, and ta da!" I jazzed my hands. "Gemma will be saved."

"Travel the roads?" Scott said a couple of pitches higher than usual. "To the *Valley*?"

"Yes. That was your plan, right?"

"No! The roads are crazy dangerous! That's why I showed you the diary!"

I gave him sceptical eyebrows. "A note of explanation might have been useful, in that case. Or, you know, walking up to me and going, 'Hey, I got connected to the Valley because I found its massive power source on these things called the roads, but don't try it, because you'll *die*.'" I tilted my head at him emphatically. "Anyway," I said, leaning back and relaxing. "I'll be fine. You're not a Road Master. I am."

"You keep saying that like it matters," he said.

"Uh, it does?"

He turned his face away. "Not as much as you seem to think."

"What do you mean?" Was this what the book had meant about needing training?

"The roads," he said. He gave a sniffly inhale, dragged his arm over his face, and sat down next to me. He'd missed a spot: one damp tear-track was still visible near the far side of his chin. "You can't travel them alone." His voice sounded strangled.

I frowned. "But the book said—"

He cut me off with a wave. "I told you. The books are wrong." He twisted his mouth. "No, not wrong, just incomplete. Look, I don't care what the books say, you can't travel the roads alone. You need a Road Master to navigate the roads, but you need someone else to move the Road Master."

My frown deepened. "*Move* the Road Master?" I needed someone to carry me? What?

Scott sighed deeply and scrubbed his hands over his face, mumbling.

"What?"

"Nothing." He stared at me, one hand still twined through his hair, gripping it like he had to hold his head to keep it on. "I—" He stopped, the sudden sort of stop that meant his mind wanted to speak but his tongue was having none of it.

I drew my knees up to my chest. In the soft glow of Sanctuary, his eyes were partially hidden, and I could almost forget the haunted look they often held. This, I reminded myself, was a boy who had seen too much. "For Gemma?" I prompted softly.

"Gemma." He deflated, releasing his hair, as though Gemma's name was some sort of charm against the tension that had filled him.

The silence ticked away, the smell of salt water ebbing and flowing with the breeze.

"You can't go near the Valley," he said at length. "Please trust me on that. Even if you're a strong enough Road Master to travel the roads—which, given what you did with the Valley before, you probably are—you can't go near the source of the Valley's power." He shifted and met my eye, sad and a little desperate. "Please. You have to trust me on this. Promise you won't go near it."

"How do you know about road mastery?" I asked so I didn't have to make another promise I wasn't sure I could keep.

His whole body tensed, shoulders hunching, jaw and fists alike clenching and twitching.

Here it came. The *real* information I needed.

"My—" He scrubbed at his face. "My mother was a Road Master."

I gaped. "Your *mother*?"

Again, he nodded.

All the disconnected pieces of information I'd carried in my head the last few months clicked into place, a Rubik's cube finally solved. "Your mother was a Road Master. She took you on the roads when you were younger,"—frogging elephants, how young? How young was he when his mother decided that her son was old enough to join her quest for darkness? Anger coursed through me, and I fought to keep my voice level—"and she found the heart of the Valley."

Another nod, more miserable than ever. Scott stared at the ground as though he might sink into it at any moment.

"And then... What? She connected herself to it somehow and it became alive?"

"She connected herself to it so she could use it as a power source. Only it works both ways, and she wasn't prepared: the Valley was stronger than she was, and it started draining her life force in order to make itself alive. She..." His hands balled in his lap and my own chest ached in response. "She died."

I remembered the double line through his mother in the list of people he lived. How much had it cost him to rule that line, to know that she was never coming back?

Then I remembered her profile; maybe he'd had mixed feelings about her death.

"I'm sorry," I said in a small voice, because what else was there to say?

He raised and dropped one shoulder, a too-simple gesture for all it contained. "Anyway," he continued, "you can't go on the roads alone. If my mum's experience is typical, you'll be able to see the path, but you'll get overwhelmed by all the information you're getting and won't be able to move your body. You need someone with you to keep you grounded. But even then, you can't go near the Valley. It's too strong, too powerful. It'd suck you right in along with Gemma, and then it would use your power to take over the world. All the worlds."

Misery pooled in my chest. I inhaled deeply; the breeze had died, leaving the air thick and heavy.

No hope. That's what Scott was saying. There was no hope for Gemma. "Why did you show me the journal?" I said, arms wrapping around my stomach to keep the despair from spilling out.

He frowned at me.

"If there's nothing we can do, if the roads are too dangerous to travel, why tell me about them?" Why torment me with the possibility of success, only to snatch it immediately away? My throat ached. "Just tell me why."

His face softened as he realised what I meant. "No," he said, touching my knee more gently than I would've believed possible. "I didn't say there's nothing we can do. I came here to talk to you because I think there *is* something we can do. But I'm not familiar with the magic of Sanctuary," he said, withdrawing his hand to flick a leaf off the rock beside him. "So I don't know if it will work."

"Aphros will know," I said immediately.

Scott nodded. "Probably." He took a long inhale, and shed the last of his grief like an old skin. The Scott I was used to seeing at school reappeared, and I wondered how often he'd had to change his skins before. He leaned over his knees. "What I *think*," he said carefully, and I realised I was wrong: this wasn't school-Scott either, but something new, something different. "Is that going to the Valley's power source is too dangerous, and disconnecting her like you did with me must also be really dangerous, or you'd have done it already."

Perhaps, I reflected as he spoke, this was Real Scott, interested and animated and logical. Now there was a thought.

"But the Valley is supposed to be a sort of mirror of Sanctuary, a yang to its yin, or something. What if Sanctuary also has a power source?" he asked, eyes alight. "If we could find that, if we could link Gem to *that*..." He shrugged, hands splayed, palms to the sky. "It might be enough to balance the pull of the Valley on her life force."

"Her soulprint," I amended automatically, and he nodded.

Balance. When I'd first met Aphros, she'd told me that I needed to restore the balance between Sanctuary and the Valley.

I nodded again, lighter. "That could work."

Aphros? I pulled on the strange thread that connected us, and felt her turn her attention to me. *Scott thinks that if we anchor Gemma to Sanctuary permanently, it would balance out the connection with the Valley and make her okay. Do you think that would work?*

A long silence, then, *Yes. That would work. Well.*

I grinned as relief flooded over me. "Aphros thinks it will work," I told Scott.

He blinked. "Did you just use road mastery to ask her? I didn't know it could do that."

"Something like that," I replied, still grinning. "You're amazing. Thank you so much."

He scowled. "Don't thank me too much yet. We still have to survive the roads, and *find* Sanctuary's power. And Gemma will have to be with us; I don't see how she can forge the connection otherwise."

The buoyant feeling faded. I frowned. "Take Gemma on the roads?" Gemma was so fragile right now; how would we take her on the roads, especially if they were as dangerous as Scott seemed to think they were?

"Can't we just... I don't know, take her to meet the avatar of Sanctuary's heart, like the glowy light pillar in the Valley?"

Scott snorted. "The Valley only had a 'glowy light pillar' because it had already leached enough energy to make itself seem alive. Unless you're planning to donate your life to the cause..."

He tensed suddenly. "Don't. Don't do that, will you. Don't give your life force to the heart, no matter what it says, okay? Just..." He stared earnestly at me. "Please don't do that."

I rocked back a little. "Whoa, chill: no sacrificial life-giving for me, okay? I promise." I sighed heavily at yet another promise I wasn't sure I would—or could—keep. I'd save Gemma any way I could, and hopefully it wouldn't come down to anyone dying—but if I had to give my life energy to Sanctuary's heart so it could manifest enough to save Gem... Well, it was Sanctuary, not the Valley, right? Making a contract with Sanctuary seemed a lot less dangerous than making one with the Valley. I'd cross that magical bargain bridge when I got to it. *If* I got to it.

"Though really," I said, "How safe is it to take Gemma on the roads in the first place? Isn't that going to be both hard and dangerous?" I tilted my head, not really sure what I wanted him to say. Of course it was going to be hard and dangerous. I still had to do it.

His gaze bored holes through me. "That's why I'm coming with you."

Right, I thought. *Okay then.* But I couldn't pretend I wasn't just a tiny bit relieved that he'd suggested it before I had to ask. Scott had done this before, and he'd survived. We could do this. We really, actually could. The smile I offered was a fragile, newborn thing, but that was how he knew that it was real. "Thank you," I said, and I meant it.

13

"I STILL DON'T see why we can't just get Gemma and go," Scott muttered to me.

"Shh," I told him as I texted Mum an apology for missing dinner. Frogging time skips. Still, arriving back forty minutes late was better than the one time I'd run into myself and fainted, or the time I'd spent the next thirty-six hours with an echo of myself haunting the corner of my eye, doing everything I did, just offset five inches to my left. Nothing more disconcerting than looking down and thinking you had twenty fingers and four arms.

Can I go check on Gemma? I texted.

"You said she's progressing fast," Scott continued as we crunched down the gravel path. The creek slunk along to our right, dark and sleepy in the dusk that was only a little bit brighter than Sanctuary's usual dim glow.

Fine, Mum replied. *Be home by 8.*

I assured Mum that I would be, tucked my phone in my pocket, and shook my head at Scott. "It's late, I'm exhausted, and from what you've said, we'll all be better off if we get a good night's sleep before we try this."

"Oh, sure, we're all gonna to sleep real well tonight."

"Hilarious," I said drily. "Look, I'm going to head over to Gemma's to see her and let them know what the plan is. I'd really appreciate it if you'd come too, since you know a lot more about the roads than I do, but I totally understand if you don't want to." My footsteps crunched onward as I waited for his response.

Scott shrugged. "I guess."

I exhaled. "Thanks."

We walked on, and by the time we got to Gemma's house fifteen minutes later, the last sliver of sun had disappeared behind the treed horizon.

I tapped lightly on the door, then cracked it open. "Hello? It's just me. Can I check on Gem?"

Mrs Caro appeared in the hallway. "Edge! And Scott!" she added, making an admirable attempt at hiding her surprise. "Please, come in."

We did, and she shepherded us to the kitchen.

"How's Gem?" I asked.

"She's okay," Mrs Caro said, her smile stretched as she slid a fancy-looking pie out of the fridge and set it on the bench. Moments later, two bowls and two spoons joined it. "Here."

"You don't have to," I protested weakly as my stomach rumbled.

Scott didn't say anything, but the way he was eyeing up the pie spoke volumes.

"Nonsense," said Mrs Caro. "When's the last time you two ate anything? How long did you spend in Sanctuary today?"

"A while," I confessed as she slid gleaming slices of lemon meringue into each bowl and pushed them toward us. I sat on one of the stools, its feet scraping eagerly over the tiled floor, and picked up the spoon.

Scott hesitated.

"Come on," I said. "Don't be shy." I shoved a giant spoonful of pie into my mouth and with the now-gooey spoon, gestured at him to sit.

Reluctantly, he did, jaw twitching, glancing over his shoulder like shadows might appear at any moment. He picked up the spoon and ran his fingertips down the length of it, feeling the weight of it in his hand. Only once he'd positioned, and repositioned, and positioned his grip again did he scoop up a gleaming mound of lemon curd, white frothy meringue perched on top like clouds.

I watched, fascinated, as he closed his mouth over the spoon like it might be fragile. He slurped the pie off, and rolled it around in his mouth.

"This," he said after he'd swallowed and was refilling his spoon, "is magic."

My lips twisted sideways in a barely-concealed grin. "Never had it before?"

Eyes still closed, he shovelled in another mouthful and spoke around it. "We don't do dessert much at my house."

Belatedly, I remembered his mum. I looked down at my own pie, appetite diminished.

A creak of wood rescued me from the melancholy direction of my thoughts: Gemma, coming down the stairs. I brightened at the thought of her walking under her own steam; the block was holding better than I'd hoped.

But my mood sank again as she entered the room: her skin was sallow, her eyes dull, her hair limp and tangled, and her whole posture defeated.

I hurried over and guided her to one of the armchairs. She sank into it and I curled up at her feet, knees against my chest.

Scott brought me the rest of my pie and sat in the other armchair—an unexpected kindness.

Even more unexpected was the fact that he leaned forward, concern furrowing his brow, and took Gemma's hand. Deftly flipping it over, he found the pulse in her wrist and stilled. "How do you feel?" he asked her.

I bit my lip. He seemed to have an end in mind, so I was happy to let him take the lead, but I didn't want to hear Gemma's answer. Either it would be a lie, and that would be terrible, or it would be the truth, and that would be worse.

"I'm... I'm fine," Gemma said breathily, clearly opting for the lie.

I laid my cheek against her knee. It felt cold and knobbly, unalive, like coats on a coat rack or a lumpy mattress. "Mrs Caro, do you have a blanket?"

"You're not fine," Scott snapped. "Stop being stupid."

Gemma sank further into the chair.

"Hey," I snapped back at Scott. "Be nice."

He cut me a glance full of razors. "She looks just like Mum did, right before... before... You know. Just before." He nodded sharply. "I need to know what she's feeling. I might be able to tell you how much time we have. But I can't do anything if she won't tell me the truth." He jerked his head at Gemma, frustrated.

I squeezed my eyes closed and pressed harder against Gemma's knee. "Gem?" I said softly. "Please tell him the truth."

Her breathing was ragged, like she'd just run the cross-country course, or... like she was dying.

Mrs Caro's footsteps drawing near made me open my eyes, and I leaned aside as she covered Gemma in a thick, fuzzy blanket, tucking it in all around her.

"I feel like garbage," Gemma said breathily.

"Any hallucinations? Voices?" Scott said sharply. Gem shook her head.

Scott released her wrist and leaned back in his chair. "That's good then. How's she look to you?" he added to me.

"Aphros and I put a kind of block around the connection so it can't grow, and it seems to be holding so far." I'd tell him later about the tiny, hair-thin cracks I could sense on the block itself—later, when Gemma couldn't hear me.

"It won't hold forever though," he replied quietly.

Mrs Caro settled herself on the arm of Gem's chair. "Any thoughts on what else we can try?"

Gem said nothing, but followed the conversation intently with her eyes.

Briefly, I filled her in on what Scott had told me and what Quoise and I had found in the library, pleased when Scott actually interrupted to correct me at one point.

When I'd finished, Mrs Caro gave one sharp nod. "Be careful."

I smiled. "Always." Sort of. Ish. I was pretty sure my debt to the universe was racking up fast, with all these false promises I kept making.

Hopefully saving Gemma from the Valley—and thereby preventing the Valley from escaping to take over the world again—would balance the sums in my favour.

We stayed for a little while longer, talking about nothing in particular, and then it was time to go. "I have to get home," I said, standing.

Scott stood too, and Mrs Caro followed, nodding. Gemma had fallen asleep in the chair, long lashes curling against her brown skin, and I tucked the blanket in tighter, smiling a little. "Love you, Gem," I murmured to her.

"So you'll try getting on the roads tomorrow?" Mrs Caro asked as she walked us to the door.

I nodded. "First thing after school."

She caught my arm gently as I exited, let Scott draw a little way ahead, and bent close to my ear. Scott and I had downplayed the danger of the roads without even needing to discuss it, but Mrs Caro had never been slow.

"I know that your road mastery lets you... do *things*," she said. "You did really well, with Scott and the shadows and all. Really well. But..." Her fingers flexed as she released my arm. "Be careful. You're going to hate me for saying this, but you're only young, Emma. Gemma... I know she's your friend, but she isn't..." Mrs Caro drew in a shaky breath. "I appreciate your help more than you'll ever know. But Gemma isn't your responsibility, Edge. Don't put yourself in danger for her sake. I couldn't face your mother."

I smiled gently. "Mrs Caro," I said. "If last year taught me anything, it's that no one is ever safe. My

Dad did the right thing when he testified. I couldn't do anything less. Mum and Dad would understand."

Mrs Caro shook her head sadly. "Be careful, Emma. Just... be careful."

I gave her a long look. "Of course, Mrs Caro. Of course."

Bah-bing. There went my debt to the universe again. But it didn't matter, because soon—very soon—Gemma would be well again. And then the rest of it wouldn't matter.

14

THE NEXT AFTERNOON, Scott and I met in the glade straight after school. Thick humidity cloyed the air, and crossing to the coolness of Sanctuary provided welcome relief.

No sooner had we arrived in the alcove than Quoise appeared from the corner of the rockery. "Psst," she said, beckoning us over.

Exchanging glances, Scott and I went.

"What's up?" I said as we neared.

"The Keeper's about to have our heads is what," Quoise replied, wringing her hands and fluttering fitfully back and forth. "What have I done?" she said, her usually high-pitched voice even higher than usual.

I shot another puzzled glance at Scott, which he returned without comment. "I don't know. What have you done?"

"Told you about the roads, that's what I've done!" She stopped in mid-air, arms flailing wildly. "And now the Keeper knows, and we are all in Very! Deep! Trouble!" This time, the look I exchanged with Scott was grim. "Do you have to be here for this?" I asked Scott. "If they sense your soulprint, there's no way they won't investigate."

"I'm not leaving." His mouth set in a determined line as he crossed his arms. "Let them come. I'll handle it."

"Mm." I pursed my lips. I had no doubt actually that he would, and even less doubt that I wouldn't like his methods. "Look," I said to Quoise. "You didn't tell me anything that Scott didn't also tell me. All we need is for you to show us where the roads begin, and then you're free to disappear."

But Quoise had passed the point of reason. She rocked back and forth in the air, arms wrapped around herself, muttering. "The Keeper suspects, of course. It would take only a nod from me, and you'd be banned from Sanctuary for life as well. Do you realise that? Do you know how serious this is?"

My stomach dropped. Quoise was supposed to be my *friend*. "What," I said sharply. "You mean as serious as my best friend being consumed by the Valley, and maybe, y'know, *dying*?" As serious as the fairies lying about whether or not I could help her, about them keeping the true purpose of my abilities from me?" I folded my own arms and narrowed my eyes. "You and Gem once told me that travelling to Sanctuary is like a beneficial addiction. The atmosphere of Sanctuary gets into your head, makes you calm and focused, and your brain likes the feeling so much it makes you a calmer, better person—and it makes you want to come to Sanctuary more. So what do you think happens when you ban people?"

Quoise shook her head. "That's not the point."

"It *is* the point. My best friend is dying, or as good as, and instead of helping her, you've tossed her out of the only place that provides—ha ha—*sanctuary* for her. And because I'm trying to help her, you're threatening to do the same to me. Seriously." I tossed my head. "Either you're going to go tell the Keeper or not, but I doubt it, because otherwise you would have just *done* it instead of warning me. So quit making threats you're not planning to keep."

Scott snorted softly, and out of the corner of my eye I caught a look of approval.

Why yes, Scott, I can stand up for myself, thanks for noticing. I was too focused on Quoise to spare him an eyeroll, but I angled myself slightly away from him.

Quoise opened her mouth, stopped, folded her arms, and scowled. "You don't understand what you're asking of me," she said. "How much trouble I could be in, even for just saying *this* much to you."

She hugged herself again. "Edge," she whispered fearfully, eyes wide, "they could kick me out of Sanctuary."

I stretched forward and held my hand palm up in front of her. "I won't let them," I said.

She sighed and stepped onto my hand, peering up at me as I brought her close. "Edge, dear, you've done extraordinary things in the short time I've known you, and I appreciate the thought, but if the Keeper wants to kick me out, there really isn't anything you can do to stop her."

"What happens if you get kicked out?"

She shrugged and turned away a little, tugging at her hair and hunching her shoulders.

"Quoise. What happens?"

She heaved a sigh and glanced up. "I won't die, if that's what you're worried about. But my magic will diminish the longer I'm away from Sanctuary."

"Oh. That... isn't so bad, is it?" Other than crossing to Sanctuary, I hadn't really seen much evidence of what fairy magic could even do.

She stared mournfully at me. "Edge. Magic is, is... Magic is like being able to hear my heart beating to know I'm still alive. And Sanctuary is my home. Where else would I go?"

Magic aside, I knew a thing or two about having your home ripped away. "I won't let that happen," I said, and even though I didn't know what I could do if it came to that, I was also telling the truth.

Scott shifted next to me. I nudged him to keep quiet, but he leaned forward until his face was level with Quoise. "You have to help us," he said. "Not for Emma, not for Gemma. For yourself. Because if you don't help us, if you do nothing and Gemma dies, or if Emma dies trying to save her, a part of you will always wonder if it might have been your fault. If maybe you'd helped, then it would have turned out differently. And although you'd try to push the guilt aside and pretend like it didn't matter, like it was nothing, it would eat you alive from the inside out until one day you broke from the strain."

Part of me wanted to punch him, because tears were coursing down Quoise's cheeks, but the part of me in control told the rest of me to shut up. We *needed* Quoise on our side—and he was right.

"Help us," he said softly. "Or at least, help Emma. Don't choose to live with the guilt."

I shivered; his words sounded personal, like he was talking to himself. *I'm sorry, Scott,* I thought. *Whatever it is, I'm sorry.*

Quoise drooped, head dropping into her hands, face pressed against her palms. "I'll show you," she said, muffled through her hands. "I'll show you where the roads begin." She drew in a shaky breath, lowered her hands, and smiled a wobbly smile. "I can't come with you on the roads, but there isn't anything else I can do anyway. I'll show you."

I remembered how to breathe, and Scott strode away, face complicated and tight. "Thank you," I told Quoise. "Thank you so much."

"For the record," she said, flitting higher into the air, "I still think this is a horrible idea. Going anywhere near the Valley is asking for trouble."

I blinked. "Oh," I said, following as she led the way to the meadow. "I'm not. We're going to try to find Sanctuary's heart," I told her as Scott tagged along behind. Deliberately, I kept my eyes on Quoise so he could have a second to right himself. "We'll link Gem to that, and the two connections should balance out."

Quoise frowned. "Really? Well, that's less dangerous, but I don't think it will work. Creatures belong to either Sanctuary or the Valley. The powers of life and death shouldn't be mixed."

"Aphros manages it," I pointed out.

That was the entire reason Aphros had been able to help me last time: as a unicorn, she was bound equally to Sanctuary and the Valley, and as such was able to come and go across the border like no other creature.

(Except that one time the Valley's power had grown, fed by Scott, leaving Aphros trapped there until I'd managed to extricate Scott from his nightmare.)

Quoise snorted. "Oh, yes. Turn Gemma into a human unicorn, then. No problem."

I shrugged. "Better than hunting down the Valley, right?"

She snorted again and didn't reply.

Quoise led us across the meadow, through the little grove of pine trees, and on to the beach. The waves shushed in the background, incessant, questioning. Where? Where? Where?

I could only hope the entrance to the roads wasn't underwater or something.

But Quoise led us to an outcropping of rocks, casting furtive glances over her shoulder toward the Lodge every so often.

"How likely are they to notice us?" I asked the after fifth time.

"Hm? What? Oh, I don't know. It depends on how busy they all are, and on how many other people are here right now."

"Other people?" Scott asked, frowning.

"Dimensions," I said. "Sanctuary exists over multiple dimensions. You can only see the people who entered from the same point you did. Prevents the place from feeling crowded."

He blinked and looked around. "How many other people are here?"

I shrugged. "Most people can't interact with it like we do. We're in the—what, ten percent?"

Quoise nodded. "More or less. About one in ten thousand of you can travel, though it runs stronger in some old families. Of those, only about one in ten are strong enough to see Sanctuary as a fully developed world. For the rest, it's varyingly substantial."

"Wow," said Scott as we made our way over the rocks toward the surf.

I sincerely hoped the entrance wasn't underwater. Getting Gem here was going to be difficult enough. "The fairies record the soulprints of everyone who visits Sanctuary," I continued, happy for the distraction and somewhat gratified by Scott's interest in it all. "But because there can be hundreds—or even thousands, I guess—of people here at once, they won't necessarily pick out your soulprint right away."

"Which is the only reason you didn't have more of a welcoming party," Quoise muttered.

"How would they have known we were coming, though?" I asked her.

She rolled her neck irritably. "We can sense you mid-crossing, if we're concentrating hard enough. And if we can sense you travelling, we can be there in the alcove by the time you're here."

"You're that fast?" I didn't mean to sound so surprised, but this week had been the first time I'd seen Quoise move faster than my walking pace.

"Yes. The time slips help too," she added.

"Wow."

Quoise disappeared behind a craggy outcrop taller than me—and didn't reappear.

I hopped off the rocks onto a tiny patch of sand, scrambled around the side of the outcrop, and peered around before I realised that she'd disappeared into a little cave.

My heart sank. I'd have to get down on my belly to crawl in there; what would we do with Gem?

"Not claustrophobic, are you?" Scott grinned and threw himself onto the sand.

"Only with you," I shot back, elbowing him aside as I raced him into the cave.

Inside, there was just room to sit without out heads bashing the rocky roof, and I peered around in the dimness cast by a ball of light in Quoise's hands. One knee pressed against Scott's and the other dug firmly against the cold rock wall. Shivers traced my spine. "We'll never get Gem in here," I said, breathing shallowly and a little too fast.

"Yeah." Scott looked grim until he noticed my face. "Hey, it's okay," he said. "I was only kidding about the claustrophobia."

"I wasn't," I said, closing my eyes and thinking spacious thoughts. "You're too close."

Quiet.

I cracked an eyelid open to see him staring at me with downturned lips. "It's fine," I said, nudging him with my knee. "I'd rather you were here than not."

Quoise cleared her throat. "Okay, I found it."

We both turned our heads toward her.

"Hands?"

I hesitated. I'd seen far too much of Scott's soulprint to ever like-like him, but we seemed to be doing an awful lot of hand-holding lately, and I wasn't really sure how Scott felt. Obviously a lot less awkward than I did; he grabbed my hand and held it tightly, and the half-smile he shot me was as complicated as my stomach felt.

I took a deep, steadying breath. Problem for another day. "What next?"

Quoise did that jerky-rocking thing again, full of nervous energy. "If I make you try to find it on your own, it'll take you hours. We don't have hours. I'll have to take you over. But I can't come with you. And you don't have Gemma. I assume you're taking Gemma?"

I nodded.

"So you'll have to come back with her. But I can't risk taking you over again. So I'll show you now and you'll have to do it yourself again next time, okay?" She wrung her hands.

"It's okay, Quoise, it's fine. I'll manage," I said, accidentally squeezing Scott's hand tighter.

It was her turn to take a steadying breath. "Yes. Yes I know you will. Now, close your eyes."

We did.

"Edge, I'm going to touch your cheek, and when I do, you should be able to sense the roads, okay? Your road mastery would usually be able to sense the roads without me—that's what it's for, after all—but in Sanctuary there are blocks, hiding them. I'm acting as a conduit for you this time to get around the block, but I can only hold it open for an instant, and then it's all on you, okay?"

I nodded.

"I mean it, Edge: I can only hold you over on the roads for a split second this time; the fairies can't stay on them any longer than regular people. You'll have literally half a second before the weight of the blocks comes crashing down on you, and you have to hold it open, or best case scenario, they'll force you back here with the worst headache you've ever had in your life."

My stomach clenched. I really didn't want to know what the worst-case scenario was. "I'm ready," I told her. "Let's do it."

Now Scott gripped my hand tightly, palm sweaty and slick. I could only imagine what memories this was dredging up for him.

Quoise fluttered to my shoulder and laid a tiny, cool hand on my skin. For a long moment, nothing happened. I opened my mouth to question her, but she pressed against me, warning me to silence.

I could feel the tension thrumming through her, running down her arm, through her hand, and into my cheek—into my blood stream, pumping around my body with my life. The energy grew and built, billowing into life inside me.

My skin tingled, energy arcing and crackling between my fingertips and over the edges of my ears. Power built inside me, a lightning storm in my chest, clouds rolling, light sparking, thunder crackling. It built and built and grew and built until my ribs strained.

I couldn't hold it, not anymore; was Quoise still holding the block open? Was this it?

Panic shot through me, flooding my system with adrenalin that through the energy storm, felt like liquid fire.

Pain lanced my cheek and I realised it was Quoise, trying to get my attention. "I'm letting go now!" she shouted.

No! I wanted to scream. *I can't do this! I can't hold it!* But I nodded, and the pressure on my cheek disappeared.

The energy of the storm coursed through me. Now I did scream. My lungs burned, my blood was on fire.

Power. So much power, and it was trying to consume me. How could anyone survive this?

"Road... mastery!" I heard someone gasp.

Instinctively I flung open my road mastery and grabbed—at what, I had no idea; I had no plan, no clue—but somewhere deep in the roaring chaos of the storm, my road mastery found an anchor— something firm, like solid ground.

I snatched at it, pulled, pulled harder.

Please. Please let me in!

Lightning sparked through the air, cracking over me—and through me.

I pulled harder at the solidness.

Something snapped.

The world around us shifted.

I gasped as my feet hit solid ground in the midst of the storm.

I stumbled forward, raising my hands instinctively to my face.

Scott snatched at my fingers, wrenching my shoulder and crushing my hand.

Wind roared. My ears hurt. I clapped my free hand over one ear; it didn't help.

Power boomed away from me, rolling outward in an expanding shockwave that rang the world like a gong.

The storm died. I had a vague sense of something shattering, someone crying out in pain.

Then, suddenly, the darkness behind my eyes blazed to life: burning ribbons of colour leading in every direction, tangling, twisting, twining—paths, every one of them, paths that I could walk.

Wonder swelled in my chest, buoyed by the energy currents. I was bigger than the world; the Earth could fit inside my heart. On these paths, I could travel anywhere. Everywhere. Allwheres.

If only I could make myself move. I inhaled, and a thousand scents filled my lungs, sweet and spicy, old and new, dry and humid, cinnamon and steel, oil and decaying leaves, roses and seaweed and sweat, sunshine and chocolate, brine, mangoes, vanilla, lemongrass, orange blossoms and ink, jasmine, lavender, rosemary.

Another sharp snap.

The world died.

Panic gripped me, and I flung my arms forward, searching for the paths that had suddenly disappeared. My breaths tore raggedly at my throat. The colours, the smells—gone. Where had the world gone? What was wrong?

I was dead. I had to be dead. Everything was dull and lifeless and gone.

A soft touch on my cheek.

Gentle fingers probing my hand.

I remembered how to open my eyes.

Oh. Not dead. I was on the beach in Sanctuary, and the waves sparkled in the dusk light and shushed on the sand. Scott and Quoise fussed around me, Quoise's wings flashing like the sky, Scott's eyes shining like tears—and none of it felt real, none of it felt alive, because I'd been on the roads—and the roads? The roads were glorious.

A green-winged form rose up from the rocks. "There," the Keeper of the fairies said. "Quoise Allesandre, former fairy of Sanctuary, you have had your last request. The girl is alive and well. Now, all three of you leave before I change my mind."

She floated in the air, stately and immoveable. "And if I ever," she added as she turned away, "find any of you here again?" She raised her sceptre over her head and lightning sparked. She smiled, a terrible, hungry thing with teeth of its own. "You *may* live to regret it. Or," she concluded, as she flew away, "you may die if you prefer."

"Come on," I said, ignoring the way the world spun as I sat up. I scowled at the Keeper's diminishing back. "Let's go get Gem."

15

WE CROSSED BACK to Earth in silence, Scott and I holding a dejected Quoise between us.

"I'm so sorry," I said. The oppressive humidity of a building thunderstorm shrank the clearing and changed the colour of the light; Quoise's wings seemed lurid and out of place.

She didn't reply, but instead flew straight to a nearby gum tree and perched high in its branches, knees to her chest, arms hugging them tightly.

"What happened?" I murmured to Scott. "How did the Keeper find us?"

"Something about you breaking through the blocks," he said, equally quiet. He stood shoulder to shoulder with me, hands deep in his pockets as we stared up at Quoise. "The Keeper dragged you back off the roads. Nearly killed you in the process," he added softly.

I tried to find some part of me that cared, but it was like it had happened to someone else, or else to someone in a story. All I could remember was the bright glory of the roads, then dullness as I returned to the real world. "Do you think she'll be okay?" I asked instead.

In the distance, thunder rumbled. It wasn't half past five yet according to my phone, and already the night was closing in, dark and foreboding.

"I hope so."

I shot him a quick glance, surprised by the apparent genuineness of his emotions.

My phone buzzed.

I drew it out of my back pocket again, and my heart jolted all the way up to my teeth. Mrs Caro. "Hello?" My pulse raced.

"What just happened?"

"I found the roads," I said, watching Scott in the dim light as he continued watching Quoise. "How's Gem?"

"Not good. Whatever you did, I think it's broken the block you and Aphros put in place. I assume you're back in Nowra now?"

"I'm in the glade," I said through the buzzing ache in my chest. I'd broken her. We'd had her holding steady, and getting onto the roads had broken her. How would she survive if we actually took her onto them? I clenched the phone until my fingertips turned white.

"Right," said Mrs Caro. "Time to find out if your plan will work. I'll meet you there in fifteen minutes."

"But—"

Scott turned to me, quizzical expression lifting his eyebrows.

"What if it doesn't work?" I whispered as I met Scott's eye. "What if it makes her worse?"

"Oh, Edge," said Mrs Caro as Scott stepped forward to squeeze my shoulder a little awkwardly. "We're *all* just doing the best we can."

"It will work," Scott murmured in front of me. "We'll keep her safe."

Thunder rippled overhead.

Quoise fluttered down and perched on my shoulder. "Is that Maria?"

I nodded mutely.

Quoise nodded once, decisively. "Then let's do this. Let's get Gemma fixed."

I closed my eyes, because it was that or collapse in a heap, totally overwhelmed by everyone's support. I cleared my throat. "Okay. See you in fifteen."

"Call your mother!" Mrs Caro said sternly, then hung up.

I set an alarm for fifteen minutes and tucked my phone away. I looked from Scott to Quoise. "Thank you," I told them, exhaling heavily. "You both..." I shook my head. They both had so much to lose by helping me—but I couldn't do it without them.

"She's my friend too," Quoise said, leaning her tiny cheek against mine.

And, shockingly, Scott nodded. "Me too. I think. Probably." He inhaled, backing away. "I need to grab something. I'll be back before they get here."

Before I could protest, he'd vanished into the bushes. I could only hope he meant it, and that he'd be back—he was just as necessary now as I was.

"Are you going to call your parents?" Quoise said after Scott's crackling footsteps had faded.

"Right." I pulled my phone back out again.

Easier to lie by text, I decided. She wouldn't hear my heart pounding or my voice trembling then.

Mum, can I stay the night at Gemma's?

"You're a bad influence on me," I told Quoise.

"Me?" she squeaked.

I nodded. "I never broke rules before Sanctuary." Of course, that had been the way to stay safe, then. And now? I rubbed my free shoulder against my jaw. Now the only rules seemed to be 'do what it takes to keep your loved ones safe'. I wasn't thrilled by this way of living.

"Ha," said Quoise. "I never did either until I met you. Maybe," she added softly, "we'd just never come across rules that needed breaking."

Did some rules need breaking? Is that how life was? It made me itch, just thinking about it. But if so, how did you know which rules were which?

My phone buzzed. *Are you going to Sanctuary?*

Which rules needed breaking? Only the bad ones, I decided. However you figured that out. *Yes.*

Is Mrs Caro going with you?

Yes. At least that was a truthful answer she'd appreciate.

Can you fix Gemma this time?

...I hope so.

Be careful, Mum texted. *Stay with Maria. Stay safe.*

Always, I replied, because that was my line. *Love you.*

Wind gusted through the treetops, bringing with it the smell of rain. The light died away, dim as twilight. Beside us, the creek chattered in the dark, whispering and chuckling.

Thunder clapped again. Any minute now the rain would break and we'd be soaked. I stepped a little further from the creek, into the shelter of the trees.

Minutes ticked by, measured by the pounding of my heart and the moaning of the wind through the treetops. Their leaves rustled and swished; branches screed against each other, making lonely calls in the early night.

My alarm blared through the glade and I jumped. Still no sign of Mrs Caro and Gem—or Scott.

I shifted restlessly.

"Shh," said Quoise. "They'll be here."

"Yeah," I said. The air pressed down on us, thick and heavy, and I shifted again as sweat trickled down from the back of my neck. Usually small insect noises filled the glade instead of silence, but now the world crouched quietly, holding its breath and waiting.

Leaves and branches crackled. I swung toward the noise, relief washing over me as I recognised Mrs Caro and Gem in the light of Mrs Caro's phone.

I pressed my palm against the rough, dark bark of a tree to steady myself: Gem was walking. Our block on the Valley's connection had broken, Mrs Caro had said, but obviously not completely or Gem would be unconscious again.

"Gem," I said hoarsely, and hugged her gently.

She squeezed me back.

Quoise landed wordlessly on Gemma's shoulder. Gem inclined her head toward the half-foot tall fairy and Quoise patted her cheek.

Now all we needed was Scott.

Before the next roll of thunder could sound, he appeared, hands deep in his pockets again and collar upturned.

"Time to go?" Mrs Caro asked.

I nodded and led the way to the middle of the glade. The air zinged with the energy of the storm. I wrapped one arm around my best friend. Mrs Caro supported her from the other side, and Scott closed the gap in the circle, forgetting to be awkward.

Wind gusted over us, pricking goosebumps on our exposed skin. We pressed close together. Tonight was a night made for not being alone.

We travelled to Sanctuary, a four-headed beast linked by our hands and our mutual need for comfort. The twilight of Sanctuary seemed light in comparison to the dark we'd left behind, but even so I couldn't shake the oily, creeping sense of dread.

"Get out," a voice said levelly.

We turned.

My mouth opened and my eyes grew wide.

The archway that led out of the alcove was barred, entirely filled with glittering, jewel-winged fairies. But these were not Sanctuary's fairies as I had seen them before; in place of their usual light, gauzy dresses, these fairies were clad in something silver and shimmery that gave the sense of being both solid and liquid at once. Most of them had sceptres, smaller versions of the Keeper's one, or orbs that glimmered like gems.

The Keeper flew from the group, gold circlet glinting in her blonde hair, emerald-green dress setting her apart from the others. Her raised sceptre was almost as tall as she was, and as thick as two of my fingers. "You have one minute to leave," she said. "Or else you will suffer the consequences."

Quoise darted forward. "Viri! Why are you doing this?"

The Keeper gave her a long look. "Quoise, they, like you, have all been banned."

Gem stiffened beside me at that.

"You of all should understand what that means."

"Forty-five seconds," Scott murmured.

I glared at him. This was Sanctuary. These fairies had welcomed and supported me since I got here, and Gemma and Mrs Caro had known them practically since birth. Sure, we were technically trespassing now, but it was *Sanctuary*. What were they doing to do? Shout at us?

"This is your final warning," the Keeper said. "Leave, and you will be preserved."

Quoise stretched out her hand. "But we need—"

"What you need," the Keeper snapped, "is to obey the rules. You know the reasons why they were written. You know what the consequences will be." She softened, voice mellowing. "Quoise. Do not make this harder than it need be."

Anxiety clawed its way down my spine. "Quoise," I whispered, barely audible. "Please, we need you."

In front of us, Quoise folded her arms over her chest and tossed back her head. "I know the reasons why these rules were made," she said loudly, eyeing off the wall of fairies. "As do we all. For protection. For safety. But those rules were broken years ago, and not by any of us here."

The Keeper laughed cruelly. "You bring that creature here into Sanctuary and dare to suggest that all of you are innocent? By his hand was the Valley woken! Through his power was Skye killed— or had you forgotten that?"

"Get ready," Scott murmured, hands still in his pockets, at odds with the tension in his voice.

I didn't seriously think they would harm us, but his unease was contagious. I shrugged uncomfortably.

The Keeper turned her back on us.

The wall of fairies tensed.

Quoise turned to us, sad and defiant and lovely. "I'm sorry," she said as she returned.

"Get down!"

I stared at Scott for an instant.

Then I saw them. The wall of fairies had raised their orbs and sceptres. White light snapped and crackled around them; the air smelled like dirt and growing things.

"Down!" I echoed Scott's shout, lunging at Gemma. We hit the ground en masse as the blinding white light shot from the fairies toward us. I cringed, bracing.

Scott stood up, something small and brown in one hand.

The shadows around Gemma roared.

Scott lifted his hands in the instant the white light streaked at us. Darkness shredded the air, and the shadows left Gemma's soulprint to flank Scott. He tilted a hand and at the last possible moment, the shadows flattened into a shield.

The light hit them.

The world thundered; the ground boiled.

Gemma shrieked—I could see her mouth open, but I couldn't hear her over the gale of magic.

Life magic—and death magic.

Clashing.

Jaw locked in fury, I snatched at Scott's wrist. How dare he? How *dare* he!

Edge? A minty-green voice cut through the chaos.

Nearly choking on my rage at Scott, I locked one hand around his wrist, grabbed Gemma in the other, and twisted away.

16

"HOW *DARE* YOU?" I shouted, flinging Scott away from me as soon as we landed. Hot tears welled and I swiped at my eyes. "After everything that's happened, why would you do that?"

All that sob story about his mother taking him on the roads and him losing his mind... It was frogging garbage, all of it. He used death magic because he liked it, plain and simple.

Scott stood where he'd landed, eyes wide.

I stepped to him, fists clenching at my sides. I got up in his personal space and resisted the strong urge to slap him. "Don't you *ever* do that again."

His shock broke into a scowl. "I saved your butt and you know it. Those fairies might have been using life magic, but it wasn't going to tickle when it hit you," he said scathingly. He lifted his chin and held my gaze. "I saved you."

"Uh, Edge?"

I brushed Quoise gently aside. "You killed an innocent creature on my behalf," I snapped at Scott. "Don't expect me to thank you for it."

"Emma!"

"What?" I snapped some more, turning. My eyes widened.

Gemma hovered a foot or so off the ground, eyes completely black and shadows sleeking around her hands and ankles and shoulders.

I rounded on Scott. "This is all your fault! You used death magic and now the shadows have her!"

"I didn't do that! Shadow magic doesn't work like that! The only way for the Valley's power to strengthen like that is through its connection to her soulprint, or if..." He trailed off as he looked around.

"If *what*?" But instinctively, my gaze followed his and I looked properly at the trees around us for the first time.

Gnarled trees, bent and twisted.

Yellow-leafed trees, with black fungal spots and oozing, dark red sap.

I sucked in a sharp lungful of air and nearly choked as swamp smell and rotten fruit hit the back of my throat.

"Do you think it's safe to move her like this?" Mrs Caro murmured.

"How did we even get here?" said Scott.

"I…" My throat was too dry to talk. *I'd* done this. *I'd* brought us here—to the Valley. *Aphros? I send to her. Are you here somewhere?*

I'd caught hold of her soulprint and followed it, just as I'd done to find Gem when she'd been stuck in the Valley; I hadn't even thought about it—it was just an instinctual response to danger.

Hooves thundered on the ground and a moment later Aphros galloped into view. She caught sight of Gemma and propped to a halt, snorting and tossing her mane.

"Aphros," I said, running to her. "I tried to come to you. That was all, I just tried to follow your soulprint like last time. I'm sorry. I'm so sorry." I buried my face in her mane for a moment, breathing in the equine smell of her body while my road mastery absorbed the minty green-and-gold of her soulprint.

My babies, she said, nuzzling me. *They took my babies so I wouldn't help you.*

"No." I clenched my fists and stepped back. "No, they wouldn't."

She gazed mournfully at me.

I inhaled deeply. We were in the Valley. Gemma was just about taken by the shadows. All of us were banned from Sanctuary, and the unicorn babies were being held hostage. "No!" I swung out wildly, punching the air—then forced myself to stand rigidly still. There would be time to get angry later.

Right now, I needed to save Gem, and much as I might hate it, I needed everyone—Scott included—to help.

"Right," I said, and my voice rang out through the trees. "Here is what we are going to do. Scott, am I right that there's an entrance to the roads here in the Valley?"

He nodded.

"Is it far?"

He shrugged. "I'm not sure. I'd need to figure out where we are first."

Aphros tossed her head again. "In the place where we first met," she said.

Scott nodded, his mouth a thin, pale line. "Not far, then. Fifteen minutes." He eyed Gem. "Maybe a little more if she won't come quietly."

I nodded back. "Right. Aphros, I'm so sorry about your babies, and I promise to help you, but do you think you could carry Gem to the roads for us first?"

She stomped her hint foot. "Of course."

"Babies?" said Mrs Caro.

"The fairies have them hostage," I said, turning to her. "Which is the next thing. After we've gotten Gemma onto the roads, there's no point in you guys waiting around, especially not here in the Valley. Mrs Caro, *technically* you're the only one of us not banned from Sanctuary, though after all this..." I gestured broadly around—and right on cue, the ground below us rumbled again. Death magic plus life magic colliding in Sanctuary had *really* been a bad idea.

Urgh. Problem for later.

"Would you be willing to go back to Sanctuary with Aphros, Mrs Caro, and try to free them?"

"Holding babies hostage?" she said, eyes glinting dangerously. "Try and stop me."

I nodded. Which left... "Where's Quoise?"

Silently, Scott pointed into the trees. Quoise huddled above a fallen log a little way away, hovering in the air in a tight fetal ball.

I exhaled heavily. "Scott, Mrs Caro, try to get Gem onto Aphros," I said over my shoulder as I went to Quoise.

"Quoise?" I called softly as I approached.

No response. This close, I could see her whole body quivering.

"Quoise, are you okay?" Stupid question, but I had no clue what else to say.

"Don't touch me!"

I crouched next to her. "Okay." I ground my teeth. I had to get Gemma to the roads, like, yesterday, but instead of getting the job done, I was stuck talking down a panicked fairy. "Are you hurt?"

Quoise drew herself into a tighter ball. "We're in the Valley. I'm not even alive right now. You're probably just an after-death hallucination."

I frowned. She might be being a little melo-dramatic, but on the other hand, she did have a point. "Quoise, you're not dead."

No response again.

"I don't think you understand," I said, bouncing a little. "Quoise, we're in the Valley, and you're *alive*."

Cautiously, Quoise lifted her head. "But Skye died. The shadows got her."

"No shadows here." I gestured absently, then frowned. For practically ever the fairies had treated the Valley and the shadows as though they were one and the same. But apparently, they were not.

Quoise bumped down onto the fallen log and startled. She stared at the log as though it might try to devour her. When it didn't, she reached a cautious hand out to test her luck further.

She looked up at me, eyes wide with wonder. "I'm alive."

I nodded.

"I'm in the Valley, and I'm *alive*."

I held my hand out to her. "Can we go save Gem now, please?"

Quoise gave herself a little shake, then shot into the air, spiralling as she flew up, up, up over the treetops. An instant later she was back, and busi-nesslike. "Let's go."

We rejoined the others and set off, Scott in the lead, Gemma riding on Aphros with Mrs Caro on one side and Quoise on the other, and me bringing up the rear.

I'd felt a moment of joy as Quoise had celebrated not being dead in the Valley, but it was soon overtaken by other, less pleasant feelings. The shadows wreathed around Gemma, invisible to everyone else but heavy and foreboding against my road mastery.

I shut my senses down to a tiny trickle, but it didn't help; the way that Gem perched on Aphros, stiff and unblinking, her stare oddly bird-like as she turned her head this way and that...

Even without my road mastery, it was impossible to forget that the body in front of me very nearly belonged to the Valley.

Fifteen minutes had never seemed so long. One heavy, trudging step after the other, we walked, the skin on the back of my neck prickling constantly as though spiders crawled through my hair. How many hours was it now since I'd gotten up this morning? I had no idea, but my eyelids felt sandy and my limbs grew heavier by the moment. At the end of this all, I was going to sleep for a week.

Eventually, though, we stopped, and I went forward to join Scott.

"Just here," he murmured.

I nodded, still annoyed at him—even if I now had even more evidence that the fairies had never been telling the truth, he'd still killed a mouse or something on our behalf.

"I'm sorry you can't come," I said to Mrs Caro as she guided Gem over to us, and I was. It would have been nice to have an adult there. But Scott had convinced us earlier in too-graphic terms that the smaller the party the better: one Road Master to navigate the roads, one normal person to guide the Road Master, and Gemma, to be healed. Any more jeopardised the safety of us all.

Mrs Caro smiled, a thin, stretched thing. "It's okay," she said. "I trust you."

I'd known that for a while—she'd trusted me to get Gemma back last time, after all—but right now, standing literally on the borders between worlds, her trust rested like iron rod across my shoulders. It suddenly felt like a very weighty thing indeed to be a Road Master, and to be the only one who could save your best friend.

I allowed myself a precious instant to hate the universe, and then I took a deep breath: this was it. I laid a hand on Scott's shoulder because I had to, gently took Gem's hand with my other, and closed my eyes.

"Wait." Scott's voice trembled, sending adrenalin pumping through my veins.

"What?" It came out snappier than I'd intended, psyched up as I was for the most dangerous journey of my life.

"I... forgot to tell you something."

Nerves trilled through my stomach. "You *forgot to tell me something*?" This time the words were exactly as snappy as I intended. I glared at him.

He squirmed. "When we cross through, there might be... things there."

I fought the urge to dig my nails into his shoulder. "What kind of things?"

He mumbled.

"Pardon?"

"Guardians, I think. They protect the roads from intruders. We might have to get past them to use the roads."

"What. Kind. Of. Guardians?"

He whispered: "I don't know." A fleeting glance at my face, ghost-like before the winds tore it away. "You'll have to concentrate."

"On what?" This was like playing cryptic crosswords with Gemma's life at stake. How could he have 'forgotten' to tell me this earlier?

He avoided my eye, shifting while his clenched jaw twitched. "You don't understand," he said. "The roads... They're different for people who aren't Road Masters. They mess with your mind, your memory. You know that, you saw the journal. My memories of the roads are all patchy and strange, out of order, like a dream." He tilted his head. "You know when you wake up after a really intense dream and you're struck with the mood and a few images you know used to make sense, but nothing to tie it all together?"

I nodded. I'd had those kind of dreams a lot, usually with images like a dead girl's body in a train station bathroom, or dark shadows chasing me through the trees.

"It's like that."

I sighed and released his shoulder long enough to pinch at my forehead. So there would be things trying to keep us off the roads; so there would be people trying to stop us from doing what we needed to do. That was hardly unusual these days. "Okay," I said while exhaling. "We'll manage. We'll both keep an eye out and hopefully we'll..." Do what? Run away? Defeat them? Did we have to fight them? I sincerely hoped not.

Mrs Caro had been watching the exchange silently, pale cheeked and tense. She opened her mouth, then closed it, then opened it again, fingers twitching similarly at her sides. "You don't have to do this," she said. "If there's a danger, if there's a risk..." She shook her head in short, jerky shakes. "I can't tell your mother that something has happened to you too."

"We'll be fine," I said firmly. "Won't we, Scott." I directed him a significant look.

He shrugged. "Sure. You're much stronger than my mother was."

Adrenalin surged through me again. Hearing other people talk about my abilities still thrilled me in some strange way; it made them real, and to know that people thought I was strong, that I was good at what I did... I nodded. "We'll be fine."

"Emma," Mrs Caro began.

"Ready?" I muttered to Scott.

"Emma, I'm not going to let you do this. I don't know what I was thinking. This is far too dangerous, and you're thirteen, for heaven's sake. This is ridiculous. We're going—"

Her words cut off like a switch, because contrary to her advice, one hand on Scott and one on Gemma, I'd entered the Roads Between.

This time, I was prepared for the power storm that surged as we entered. I let it rush through me, filling me with light. It still hurt—but now that I knew what waited for me once the pain was over, I could bear it a lot more easily.

Sure enough, the power soon burst away in a circle of sound and light, like someone had rung the world—and we were on the roads.

17

COLOURS AND SMELLS and sounds swirled around me, mesmerising this time rather than overwhelming. The sensations seemed to ebb and flow: now the high, silver tinkling of bells and chimes, then raucous squawking like parrots or maybe someone dragging a saw over tortured metal.

Blues and greens flashed around as though we were underwater in a cool, clear pond; they gave way to the hot oranges and soft pinks of a sunset, before fading to deep blackness, studded with firework-flashes of green.

I smelled cut grass, dirt, hot concrete, baking cookies, melted chocolate, burnt chemicals, wet dog, something floral. I stood, frozen in place by the gloriousness of it all. As before, trails of colour led away in every direction: forward, backward, left, right, even up and down. I could stare forever.

Something prodded me in between my shoulder blades, and a sharp pain squeezed my fingers. It reminded me of the frustrated gesture of someone who'd been trying to get my attention for a long time—and sudden realisation percolated down through the sensory stimulus: Scott. Scott was here with me, and he wanted my attention.

I turned, light-blind, searching for him. Nothing. Not in any direction. Just constant, firm pressure on my hand, as though nothing short of death or dismemberment would induce him to let go.

I could feel him, but not see him. Why?

A glimmer of stars resolved in the current blackness, a localised patch of night sky and velvet. Next to it, the smell of vast hilltops at night, the feel of cold autumn winds, and a dark, starless sky. Scott. Gemma and Scott. I couldn't see them, but I could see their soulprints. Smiling, I squeezed back at Scott's invisible hand.

His grip relaxed a fraction: relief. I couldn't see him, but we could manage basic communication at least. I wondered if he could see me.

Right. So the next thing to do was choose a path, I supposed. But which one? I didn't even know what the heart of Sanctuary looked like, let alone where it might be. Scott had said to use my road mastery, just like when I was searching out a person, but I couldn't see anything that seemed like it might belong to Sanctuary.

The darkness brightened to tropical greens and yellows. Sounds like torrential waterfalls rose and fell around me, and the smell of charcoal drifted by. I closed my eyes and inhaled deeply. Ice crystals on the wind. Eucalypts breathing under a hot summer sun. Stagnant water. Lavender.

A tug at my hand brought me back to awareness. Urgh. I'd gotten lost in the roads again. "Focus, Emma," I muttered.

I gazed around, and suddenly adrenalin spiked through my veins. I retraced my metaphorical steps, combing the roads with all my senses, wondering what had prompted it.

There, again. A flash of darkness off to the right; a deep, booming pulse like a kettle drum; and underneath all the other sounds, a slowly building note, long, drawn-out, and getting louder.

I swallowed.

There are things on the roads.

Scott's grip convulsed around my fingers; he'd seen it too. All I could see was its soulprint: dark, black, empty, with the glimmer and heat of fire inside. My hairs stood on end and my pulse raced. I couldn't decide whether it would be worse to see the creature itself—who knew what nightmares it would conjure?—or to see and feel this, because the creature's soulprint wasn't just sight and warmth; like all soulprints, it was a multidimensional thing, with elements from all my senses, and right now

161

every one of them was screaming the same thing to me in a hundred different ways: Run. Flee. Get away. Now.

"How do I fight this, Scott?" I whispered through dry lips. "What do we do?" *I don't know what to do. I don't even know where I am.*

The booming note came again, and the building shriek in the background was nearly loud enough to drown out the chiming of the roads. Beside me, Gemma's soulprint shifted. My stomach dropped as I realised that it was dissipating, bleeding out into the air around us.

No, not the air around us; it was bleeding toward the presence, the thing, the menace that was trying to warn us off the roads and away.

No. I had not come this far for something to steal away Gemma's soul now, not when we were here, when we'd made it to the roads, and we were so darned close.

I grabbed tightly onto Scott's and Gemma's fingers and clenched my teeth. Then I did something that felt a lot braver than it really must have been: I closed my eyes.

It was habit, mostly—I could see the soulprint right in front of me with my eyes open, so I didn't actually expect closing them to help—but I did it anyway, and it felt like turning my back on a monster you knew was coming, with inch-long claws and jaws full of teeth, and you knew it was going to pounce any second but you didn't know when—and I did it anyway, ignoring the fact that my breaths were coming in ragged gasps, because I couldn't let my friends die, I couldn't, and I'd saved them before, and I was going to do it again.

I'm not afraid, I told myself. Or if I am, it doesn't matter.

Eyes still closed, I sent my road mastery senses questing toward the beast, or guardian, or creature, and the world around me sparkled silver. It felt like moving through curtains of cellophane, startling and beautiful and noisy and impossible to hide.

Hide.

Gemma's soulprint stopped dissolving. The creature swung toward my road mastery sense, or where I felt like it was, several paces out in front of me. My road mastery was noisy here; I couldn't examine anything without drawing attention.

And apparently here my road mastery was tangible, something I could separate from myself.

I could draw the guardian away.

We could hide.

I flexed my grip on Scott's hand and raised our knotted fist a little, bending my knees, ready to run.

Carefully, slowly, I let my sense of road mastery continue off to my right, away toward the creature, crackling and swimming and glittering through silver fog.

"One," I murmured. *Please let this work.*

"Two." Gemma's soulprint was still hazy, partially dissolved around the edges.

"Three!" I leapt into a dead run, heading along a shining green path of light that smelled like fire and felt like rain.

Scott and Gem followed.

For a heart-pounding moment I thought we'd done it, that we were free, the strange and horrible guardian left behind with my road mastery senses.

But then another fire-hearted darkness reared up at us from below. The air left my lungs; suddenly it felt like my body and brain weren't connected any more, and abandoned, my body had forgotten how to breathe, or pulse, or move.

My road mastery. I'd left it too far behind.

Blackness closed in over my vision, and silence crept into my ears. Something tugged at my hand (perhaps?) and fire flashed under my feet.

A scream. Was that a scream? Was I screaming, or someone else? Where was I? I felt wrapped in cellophane, but my hand hurt, and it was too hot, like I was sitting in a fire, and my insides were melting.

Something, out there in the darkness, something glittery and silver and wreathed in fog. It seemed familiar, like it had once been mine. I reached out, and it came.

The darkness took over.

At least it was quiet.

18

THE SOUND OF sobbing was the first thing I recognised. "I'm sorry," a voice said. "I'm sorry! Please just let her live!"

I touched my fingers to my eyelids and realised they were closed. My body felt soft and floaty, and I had the discomforting realisation that I wasn't actually lying *on* anything. To avoid thinking too hard about that, I opened my eyes. Two dark shapes leaned over me, one dark grey, the other dark blue.

Then I realised the dark blue one wasn't actually leaning over me so much as leaning against the dark grey one for support, and I remembered. "Is she okay?" Their actual faces resolved in front of me. I tried to reach for Gemma's cheek. Something held my fingers tight. I glanced down. Oh. Scott.

He followed my gaze and hurriedly let me go. "Are *you*?"

I brushed Gemma's cheek lightly. "I'm fine."

I should probably check if that's true or not, I thought. But surprisingly, I did seem fine. The disconcerting feeling of being torn in two was gone, and the panicked fear that the guardians of the roads had created was gone, leaving a nagging sense of anxiety and being watched, but nothing else.

"I actually am," I said, looking at Scott. "Are you?"

He swallowed before nodding. "She seems to be okay too," he said, tilting his head toward Gemma gently. "What... what happened?"

I frowned. "Didn't you see them?"

His jaw twitched. "Nightmares."

I pressed my eyes closed. "Don't tell me."

"You mean you *didn't* see them?"

"No. I couldn't even see you guys. Wait." I struggled to sit. "Why can I see you? Where are we? Why aren't we still on the roads?"

Scott glanced around nervously and licked his lips. "Actually, I was hoping you could tell us where we were. Last I knew, we were on the roads, and one of those... things... came at us, and you dragged us off running, but another one jumped up from below... And then nothing. This." He gestured to the uniform greyness around. "I thought you were dead," he added softly.

I forced a bright smile over my lips. "Never." But I pulled my knees up to my chest and hugged them anyway. "Did I..." I didn't know how to finish that. Did I seem all here? Had I been unconscious long?

None of that was quite right anyway, because what I really wanted to know was, had I actually separated myself from my road mastery ability, and if so, had it hurt me permanently? And, most importantly, was this something that could help me fix Gem?

I glanced at Gem. She stared back, silent and a little glassy-eyed, but more alert than she'd been in a couple of days and without the black-eyed stare of the Valley. "Are you with us?" I asked softly.

She gave a quiet, careful nod, and my heart trilled joyfully.

I gave her a tight, one-armed hug. "Love you," I murmured.

"You... too."

Gemma was going to be okay. I was okay, Scott was okay, we weren't in immediate danger, and Gemma was going to be okay, because I would succeed at this or die trying. I took a deep, stabilising breath and looked around. "Okay," I said. "Problem solving time. Clearly we aren't on the roads anymore, because a) I can see you both, and b) there are no monstrous guardian things, and c) I'm not overwhelmed by soulprints anymore. So question one: Where are we?"

Scott narrowed his eyes at me. "You have follow up questions to that, don't you?"

I blinked. "Of course I do. Question two: How did we get here? Question three: How do we get back? Question four: Do we *want* to get back? Et cetera. Want me to keep going?"

He shook his head in mild disgust. "I'm not saying it's not a good thing," he said, "keeping your head in a crisis. But really. You take it to the extreme."

I rolled my eyes. "Grey," I said, gesturing around. "Absence of sensory input. I'm guessing some sort of pocket existence off the roads?" I stood up and arched my back. "The roads connect different realities, right?"

Scott nodded.

"So we're in a different one. We've slipped off the roads. Yes?"

He shrugged. "Seems plausible."

I reached up to crack my shoulders—and my fingers brushed against something solid. I jerked my gaze up, but I could only see grey, grey and more grey. Carefully, I reached out my fingers again. Solid. "Hmm."

"Hmm what?" Scott said, scrutinising my hands.

"There's some sort of barrier here." I tested out a couple of steps, fingers trailing over the ceiling that wasn't cool or warm or soft or hard, just... solid.

Like the floor, I realised, and stooped to check. Sure enough, there was that same weird sensation of solid nothingness. "How big do you think this place is?" I said. It was the kind of infinite grey that could have gone on forever, or—I halted. Or there could be another wall just a meter or so away. And a corner. And another wall.

Quickly, I sketched out the bounds of our new world: about three and a half large paces square, and just tall enough for me to comfortably reach the roof. "Okay that's weird," I said, and told the others what I'd found. "What's the point of a world that's like, ten square meters?" I frowned.

"Experiment gone wrong?" Scott chirped.

I rolled my eyes again. "Genius. Thanks."

Gem inhaled. "It's... It's the only thing I could think of," she said. "Sorry."

I blinked. "You brought us here?"

She nodded carefully. "I... travelled."

"Gem, you genius!" I hugged her gently. "Well," I said, "that solves that mystery. But now how do we find the roads again?" I pressed my hand against the not-wall again, thinking, feeling. I frowned. "I think there's something through here." I reached out with my road mastery.

My stomach lurched, thick and queasy as my road mastery extended away. Quickly, I reeled it back in. I pressed my hand against my belly and grimaced. Okay. So, taking it easy then.

Carefully, I tried again, reaching out slower than I'd even thought possible. My road mastery bumped up against the wall of our new world, and for a moment I thought that would be it—but then they slipped through a shimmering net of resistance like a fish popping through jelly, and I gasped.

The roads were right on the other side. And so was my road mastery. I breathed deeply to still the panic and reeled my senses back in, panic easing as they reconnected with my body.

What would've happened if we had fallen off the roads, and my road mastery had stayed behind?

Nausea rolled through my stomach, and I opened my eyes, recollecting myself. "Roads are through here," I said, tapping the not-wall.

"Should we keep going?"

I raised an eyebrow at Scott. "Or what? Sit here for the rest of forever?"

It was his turn to roll his eyes. "Or do you need a break. You were just unconscious on the floor for five minutes, after all."

I shrugged. "I'm fine." My stomach was fine too. No nausea at all. Nope. Not even a bit. No siree. "Besides," I said with a significant glance at Gem.

With a sigh of long-suffering, Scott dragged himself to his feet, then helped Gemma up.

I gave her a tiny smile—it was so good to see her on her own two feet. "How are you feeling?"

She nodded carefully. "Better."

I squinted at her. The cord that connected her to the Valley hadn't changed, but at least she wasn't going wild on us again. "Good."

I squared my shoulders and inhaled. "Over here, you two." I offered them my hands, palms up.

Together, they reached out and laid their hands in mine. I stared for a moment at the tangled knots our fingers made together.

"Wait, shouldn't we have some kind of signal or something?" said Scott.

My eyebrows twitched upward. "Good idea. One squeeze for danger, two squeezes for run, that sort of thing?"

He nodded, a little grim. "Okay, one squeeze for danger, watch out. Two squeezes if any of us see something that's unusual but not dangerous. Three squeezes means run like the blazes."

"And we can twist our hands like this," I said, rotating our knot of fingers, "to indicate direction."

They both nodded.

"Are you sure you're going to be okay to walk?" I said to Gem. "I have no idea how long it could take. We pretty much just have to walk until I can sense something Sanctuary-ish." Her face wasn't quite so pale as it had been, but it was still several shades lighter than its usual mid-brown.

She shrugged.

Scott gave her a long, considering look. "I think I'd better carry you."

She squirmed and shook her head. "You can't... Too heavy... Not the whole way." She turned her gaze on me, desperate for my support.

I bit my lip. "I don't know, Gemma. Why don't you let him give you a piggyback for a bit or something?"

Her eyes shone wetly, and I sighed. "You know what? Just walk for a bit. We'll be okay. If we run into more of those guardian things, I know what to do to distract them now, and if that doesn't work I'm sure you can just travel us into another helpful world for a rest."

"I'm sorry," Gemma whispered, and I realised my tone had been more cutting than I'd intended.

"No," I said, pressing my forehead against her shoulder. "Don't be. It's okay." I breathed slowly in, then sharply out, trying to dispel the unease in my gut. "We'll be fine." Hopefully she didn't notice the rubberiness of my smile.

I inched forward until my toes touched the not-wall of our grey, misty world, and closed my eyes. "Hold tight, guys," I said, squeezing their hands. "Roads Between, round two."

The pain seemed to pass a little faster this time, the power build up and release more predictable, more bearable. I could see how someone might get used to this to the point where it felt like nothing.

The sensory overload was just as intense though, and like last time, I couldn't see my friends once we were back on the roads. But I could see their soulprints, strong and contained beside me—no leaching out this time.

The black cord of the Valley's hold on Gemma stretched away into nothingness, and I stared at it until I felt a strange rippling pressure on my fingers.

I looked down. One for danger, two for interesting, three for run. Where did weird rippling rank on that scale?

Oh, right. Move. I had to start moving again.

I looked around, hoping for a clue as to which direction we should go. No strange, dark creatures this time, which was great, but there was nothing else to show the way either.

I ripple-squeezed Scott's hand back, and held my lip between my teeth to one side. Often when I'd been looking for things before, it had been my road mastery that had shown the way. When I'd been in the Valley's sinkhole a few weeks back, I'd navigated by following traces of Gemma's soulprint. But here there was nothing to distinguish one path from another, and no one we knew had been here before. Well. No one I knew.

Lights played all around me, magenta and candy pink and pale lemon and autumn red, ghost gum grey and ocean blue, pale, baby green and a flash of bright, glowing gold.

Sounds: The roar of the ocean, traffic horns, something metallic clinking softly, a violin melody, whispers against my face.

Smells: Burnt sugar. Tar. Mud. Roses. Laundry powder. Mint.

Sensations: Fire-warmth. Pins and needles. Cold steel. A soft, careful breeze on my cheeks.

I blinked, trying to detangle my thoughts. Somewhere in that litany of sensations was a thread of something familiar. Something, somewhere... I scanned the roads again. What was it? What had I recognised?

A flash of gold.

Mint-green freshness.

A breath of wind whispering against my face.

"Aphros?" I whispered. But surely she couldn't be here, hadn't been here; she'd been just as naive about the roads as we had.

Scott rippled his fingers against mine, more urgently this time.

Movement. I had to move, or the sensations of the road would crowd into my mind and paralyse me—a heavenly paralysis, but paralysis nonetheless.

Mint green and bright gold. Soft, gentle breezes. Maybe Aphros had been here before, maybe she hadn't, but right now, it was all I had to go on, and it was as good as anything else, and a lot, lot better than nothing. "Okay," I told my friends, even though they couldn't hear me. "Let's go."

19

UNFORTUNATELY, THE WAY forward seemed largely in parallel with the Valley's cord, stretching away at Gemma's soulprint—and the longer we walked, the stronger it became. At one point, Scott tugged me to a stop, and there was a briefly confusing kerfuffle—until I realised that Gem had given in, and Scott was piggybacking her after all.

My right hand felt empty without her.

Several times—okay, maybe more like several times a minute—Scott had to tug on my hand to remind me to keep moving—the roads were utterly mesmerising, and glorious.

But eventually we reached a place where the trail that seemed like Aphros petered out and something warm and golden pulsed beneath my feet. I crouched, trailing my fingers over—whatever it was we were standing on. I didn't want to think too hard about that one, because while we'd been walking, the trail had sometimes lead directly up or twistingly down, and it seemed like directions here were somewhat... flexible. I didn't want to meditate on what was or wasn't holding us up, and whether it would or wouldn't continue to do so.

Scott jiggled at my hand again, and I squeezed back twice. *I see something, not dangerous. Give me a second.*

I tilted my head from side to side, trying to figure out what was different about this particular patch of road. Because apart from the fact that the trail that looked like Aphros had disappeared, and the pulsing warmth beneath us, something seemed... brighter, maybe. Sharper. I looked around and realised that in fact, everything *was* sharper—including Scott and Gemma's soulprints. Something was sharpening my road mastery here, making it even stronger than before. I closed my eyes, trying to focus, but it was hard with the sensory overload of the roads constantly tugging at my awareness.

The smell of steel. A glint of copper. Old paper rustling. The weight of books in your hand. Sunlight through green leaves. The smell of snow-sharp air.

Focus.

A heartbeat, subtle but persistent. Sparkling golden light. Vivid red. The texture of linen. Grey stone. Cinnamon and spice.

Focus!

Rushing water. Pipes rattling. Melted cheese. Thick, silky fur. Brilliant, blinding white. The persistent heartbeat.

FOCUS!

The heartbeat. Golden light.

I'd helped Aphros restore the balance earlier in the year when Scott's association with the heart of the Valley had nearly torn the worlds to shreds, and I'd seen the balance as a giant, writhing ball of gold and black light.

Gold light. Golden in exactly the way of the warm, pulsing glow beneath our feet.

Was this the heart of Sanctuary, then?

I knelt down and peered at it, one hand still firmly anchored in Scott's. It seemed likely that this *was* the heart of Sanctuary, but if so, how did I get to it? The heart of the Valley had been much easier to access; I'd just walked into the giant black cloud of nothingness, then walked until I'd found the pillar of dark light.

Of course, the Valley had already been embodied in Scott by that point.

Hmm. Scott. How had *he* gotten to the heart of the Valley? If only I could talk to him properly and ask him. If only I'd thought to ask before. That's if he remembered, which he probably didn't. I clenched my jaw in frustration and drummed my fingers on the not-ground.

Warmth from the heart radiated up to me, suffusing me with peace and happiness. Definitely Sanctuary. I'd figure this out yet.

Maybe I didn't have to get to the actual heart; maybe I could reach it from here somehow, and convince it to attach to Gemma.

I shook my head. I couldn't see any other option right now, so I might as well give it a go. I put steady pressure on Scott's hand, trying to encourage him to sit. After a confused moment or two, he got the idea and I watched as his soulprint sank down next to me. Gemma seemed to disentangle herself from him, and after another moment I felt the pressure on my hand change. I smiled, and squeezed Gemma's hand gently. She squeezed back, and a little bit of relief loosened the tension across my shoulders.

Well, I thought, taking a deep breath, here goes nothing. Closing my eyes, I stretched out for Gemma's soulprint and the thick black cord woven into it. Bile rose in the back of my throat as I brushed against the Valley's cord, the smell of rotten fruit cloying my senses. Swallowing hard, I contemplated the fabric of Gemma's soulprint, wondering how I was going to connect it to the golden heart below me.

I wish Aphros was here.

Carefully, holding Gemma's soul-print as though in one hand, I extended the other part of my road mastery down to the warmth below. It bumped against something solid, clear and see-through but preventing me from getting to the heart nonetheless.

But there, just ahead, swirling in the heart, the fresh scent of mint.

Last time, I'd gotten to Gemma by twisting sideways through dimensions and following her soulprint. I'd followed Aphros the same way. Was it possible I could do the same thing to get into the heart of Sanctuary?

Nothing else to try. Before I could think it over any further, I tightened my grip on Gemma and her soulprint, and twisted.

Nothing happened.

I frowned. For a split second there, it had felt like it was going to work, but then something had... caught. Like there was a glass floor between us and the power of Sanctuary, and part of us had passed through, and part of us had been trapped by the glass.

I frowned at Gemma's soulprint. I was pretty sure I had a good enough grip on it; it had to be something else.

My eyebrows released their tension as I realised it was the Valley-cord that had squirmed away from Sanctuary's warmth. If the fairies weren't going to let Gemma into Sanctuary any more because of her taint, how did I expect to be able to pull the taint directly into the magical heart that made Sanctuary what it was?

I scrunched up my face. *Stupid, stupid.*

I allowed myself one long inhale, followed by an explosive exhale.

Right. Now we solve this. I am going to save Gemma, and you, Valley, are not going to stop me.

I'd gotten around the Valley's power before. I could do it again.

Okay. But *what* could I do? Together, Aphros and I had been able to separate Scott from the Valley's power, restoring the balance between Sanctuary and the Valley. But how did that help with Gemma? The whole point was that I couldn't just cut her free. I chewed my lower lip. I was missing something still, something obvious.

Gemma's grip on my fingers shifted, a casual movement that drew my eyes back to her soulprint, the glorious pattern of diamond-like stars studding velvet of the deepest night. The Valley's cord hadn't thickened since we'd gotten onto the roads, but its feelers had spread, integrating itself further through the warp and weft of her identity.

If the darkness spread, my best friend would die.

Abruptly, loneliness consumed me. Only I could see the beauty of the roads around me, feel the pulsing of the heart of the Valley, see the soulprints of my friends and the truth of who they really were—but not their faces.

And here, not a single person could see me. I was invisible, non-existent except for a tenuous touching of fingers, and I was alone. No one else could help me.

I bit my lip again, small, rapid bites that worked the threat of tears away.

My road mastery drifted around us, scanning, and I felt myself being drawn into the roads again.

No, I told myself. *You have to stay focused. You have to do this.*

But I couldn't do it alone. Once again, I wished Aphros was here. Wishfully, I tugged at the strange soulprint connection I had with her.

An answer came back, faint and distant. *Hello?*

I stiffened. *Aphros? Is that you?*

What do you need? I am… occupied.

The twins. I squeezed my eyes shut and hoped they'd be okay. *I found the heart,* I told her. *But I can't get in using my road mastery.*

Seeds, she sent back. *Use their magic.*

The connection lengthened and drifted.

Aphros? Aphros, can you hear me?

Nothing.

I took a deep breath. Okay. Seed magic, I could do that. I dug into my pocket—and fear caught at my throat. My seeds were gone. Some time in all the running and trudging and twisting, the packet had fallen from my pocket, and now it was gone.

I slumped.

Scott rippled along my fingers again. *Move.*

I squeezed back, two squeezes and one good long one that I sunk as much *wait* into as I could.

His soulprint shifted impatiently beside us, a flicker of cold starlight licking at the vast emptiness within him.

Darkness. He was so full of darkness. No wonder the Valley had found him convenient prey. No wonder he'd taken so well to death magic.

My breath caught. Death magic. No, what had Scott called it? Shadow magic. Because you didn't have to kill something to use it. You just had to make a sacrifice.

I'd done it once before to get into the Valley, when Scott was nearly lost to the shadows for good. Instead of killing anything else, I'd used myself— my own blood.

I turned and stared at the heart of Sanctuary. Could I do it? I'd used life magic inside the heart of the Valley; logically, then I should be able to use death magic inside the heart of Sanctuary.

If I dared. Did I dare?

Scott had used death magic—*shadow* magic— earlier in Sanctuary, and the world had rocked. Had that been because he'd used shadow magic in Sanctuary, or because of the clash between shadow and seed magic?

If I didn't dare use shadow magic, could I sacrifice some of *my* life, perhaps? That would still be life magic, wouldn't it? But try as I might, I couldn't think of a way to do that which didn't involve blood—which was shadow magic.

I sighed. It didn't matter whether using death magic in the heart of Sanctuary was right or not; it didn't matter whether using it at all made me a terrible person or not. All that mattered was that it was the way to save my friend.

With no other way to draw blood, I took one fingernail between my teeth, braced myself, and tore. My heart thundered in my chest and I cried out around the broken nail: it *hurt*.

The sound of rain rose around me, the smell of water, the feel of clean, fresh droplets running down my face.

I closed my eyes, tightened my grip on Gemma's hand, and let my road mastery flow into the blood that dribbled down my finger. Then I twisted. And this time, it worked.

20

"WHERE... WHERE ARE we?"

Gemma's faint voice made me realise my eyes were still closed—it was easy to forget, considering the roads looked pretty much the same either way—and I opened them.

Wow. The roads might look the same either way, but the heart of Sanctuary definitely did not. Where the heart of the Valley had been pretty much the Black Sinkhole of Doom, the heart of Sanctuary was like standing in a round chamber full of sunshine; the curved walls glowed and the floor was so bright it was like walking on light.

And even better, Gemma stood next to me, now visible, blinking bewildered at the golden light around us.

I shot Scott a look of relief, which he promptly returned. We'd made it.

Calmness infused me, and the golden light glowed more intensely than ever before; this was the heart of Sanctuary, and we'd made it in. I squeezed Gemma tightly.

"I can see you," she said. "Why?"

A smile lit my face; it felt even brighter than the golden fire of Sanctuary's heart. "We're here," I said. "We're in the heart of Sanctuary."

Relief softened her shoulders and the lines of her face. "We... made it." She closed her eyes and swallowed. "What... What now?" she asked.

I took her hand again. "Now we fix you."

"Can... Can I sit down?"

"Of course." Scott and I helped her down, and I squeezed her shoulders. *Here goes nothing,* I thought. Time to save my best friend. "I'm not sure what this will look like," I told Scott. "Or how long it will take."

He nodded and lay down flat on the floor. He must have been exhausted after carrying Gemma for so long. Death magic or no, I wouldn't forget that.

I sat down next to Gem and breathed deeply. The light of Sanctuary's heart seeped in, filling me to overflowing; nothing else could matter right now. I would do this—I couldn't not, not here, not in the very heart of Sanctuary's power. Eyes closed, I drew up my road mastery and examined Gemma's soulprint. There, right where the Valley's power anchored itself in her soulprint, but on the other

185

side; that's where I would need to join her to Sanctuary. "I'm not sure what this will feel like for you," I told her, eyes still closed. "But I imagine you'll need to agree to it in some way, like you did with the Valley. Is that okay?"

"Of course," she murmured.

I squeezed her hand instinctively, then rolled my neck and exhaled, focusing. *Thank goodness I don't have to try to do this on the roads,* I thought. The distractions there had been almost impossible to ignore, but here Sanctuary's warm light drowned every-thing else out, and it was easy to concentrate. I reached toward the heart. Somehow, I would need to spin it into a cable, like the Valley, and attach it to Gemma.

A loud pop echoed around the golden chamber.

I whirled toward it—as did Scott, leaping to his feet.

I gaped. There, in the middle of the round chamber, was Sanctuary's Keeper, eyes closed, an intangible wind ruffling her hair.

A smile crossed her face, and when she opened her eyes and saw me, it turned vicious. "Hello, Emma Tanning."

My pulse thundered. Would she try to shoot more magic at me? I couldn't assume Scott would have another convenient mouse in his pocket.

(Oh, so *now* the mouse was convenient?

Shut up, self, I commanded. *Shut. Up.*)

"Hello."

Energy crackled around her fingers, lightning silver and sunray gold. "I suppose you know why I'm here."

I nodded, throat dry.

"How, though?" Scott asked. His voice was level and calm, but his fingers twitched at his sides.

And he had a good point.

The Keeper's smile became a shark-toothed grin. "Oh, come now. You are smart children. What else would I be Keeper of, if not the very heart of Sanctuary itself?"

That... made annoying sense. I stood, fuelled by rage at her selfishness. "You... You cow," I spat. "You knew there was a way to save Gemma. You knew this place was here, and instead of helping, you kicked us all out! Why?" I clenched my fists. "Did it make you *feel good*?"

The Keeper scowled, a fleck of lightning sparking at me. "No," she said as I ducked. "I'm not doing this because of how I *feel*. Unlike everyone else in this room, I am an adult. No." She raised her hands and power arched between them. "I did it because Gemma made her decision when she agreed to the Valley's bargain. You all made your choices," she sneered. "Gemma chose her path. She must be made to live with the consequences. Or," she added as the lightning concentrated over her right hand, "she can die with them."

The lightning speared toward us.

Gemma screamed.

"No!" Scott leapt forward, straight into the path of the lightning. It hit him square in the chest and he crumpled to the floor.

I cried out and stretched my arm toward him, torn between protecting Gem and making sure he was okay.

His chest rose and fell. Thank goodness.

He'd taken a bolt of lightning for us. Scott, bane of my existence and one-time embodiment of the Valley of Death, had *taken a bolt of lightning* for us. The world was quite possibly ending.

The Keeper pursed her lips. "Not my intended target," she said casually, "but hardly a great loss."

I shook my head. "I don't get it. If you have all this power, why let him get involved with the Valley in the first place? Why let it go as far as it did? Skye died, and you did nothing! If I hadn't broken your precious rules, he'd have been possessed by the Valley and the shadows would have been free!"

Pop.

Abruptly, there were two fairies in the centre of the room, the newcomer a dark-haired fairy with glimmering blue wings—Quoise.

I gasped.

"How in the world..." said The Keeper, beginning the question that I was also wondering. How had Quoise gotten here? She couldn't travel the roads, and she wasn't the Keeper—so how?

"I followed you," Quoise said to the Keeper. She raised a sceptre from behind her back and gave a wicked grin. "You left the Forbidden Chamber open and I came through after you. I've always wondered what was in there." She shot me a defiantly proud wink.

A Forbidden Chamber? My chest burned with pride. Good for Quoise.

The Keeper eyed the sceptre warily. "Put that away before you hurt someone."

Quoise's face lit up. I had to give her that: usually the meekest and mildest creature imaginable, she could pull off terrifying glee when it mattered most. "That's the point."

The Keeper sneered at her. "Put it away, and go home. As your Keeper, I command it."

"No," Quoise replied. "You banned me. You're not my Keeper any more."

"Then you have even less right to wield the magic. Put it away!"

Lightning sparked and crackled as Quoise lifted the sceptre over her head. "Oh," she said. "Didn't I mention? I found something else in the Forbidden Chamber."

The sceptre swirled over Quoise's head.

Magic leapt and crackled, and dread prickled my neck. Something was going wrong.

"The Book of Laws was there," Quoise said softly. "The *original* version. Any fairy may wield the lightning in a state of emergency."

"Not when the state of emergency is that fairy's doing!" the Keeper snapped, dodging a flash from Quoise's sceptre.

"Exactly," Quoise said, any trace of humour dropping away as she squared off against the Keeper.

Around us, the walls creaked and groaned. I quested out with my road mastery—and withdrew immediately. Too much magic. The entire heart of Sanctuary was overloading.

The balance. Any moment now the balance would crumble, taking this place—and us—with it.

"And this emergency is your doing," Quoise was saying to the Keeper. "I read the book, Viri. Someone's been breaking a lot of rules lately. But it wasn't us. It was you." She hefted the sceptre.

"Quoise, no!" I shouted, lunging at her too late.

Lightning flashed, silver and gold, and under the deafening roar a whine began, building, building, higher, louder.

The lightning hit the Keeper just as she released a stream of energy from her hands. It shot past Quoise's lightning arc. The walls shook.

I flung out my road mastery at the fairies and found the thread that connected them back to Sanctuary's real world.

With all the strength I could muster, I pulled at the connection.

"Come on," I muttered. "Come on!"

I pulled harder, straining as magic whirled around the room, a giant storm of pressure and power and light and sound.

Come on!

21

SNAP.

The connection broke. The fairies disappeared. I collapsed back onto the floor, panting—and realised that Gemma was lying still and silent.

Across the room, Scott stirred.

"Come on, Gem," I said, brushing her hair from her cheek.

She blinked with exaggerated slowness; some of my tension eased. Alive. Time to do this then.

Gripping Gemma's hand firmly in mine to anchor myself, I stretched for the heart of Sanctuary. My road mastery sank deeper and deeper into the light, and my worries fell away as Sanctuary's magic filled me to the brim with peace and joy and light.

But there seemed no way to hold it all, nothing to grab onto. How could I spool it out into a thread like this? How could I connect it to Gemma? The Valley had been sentient when Gemma had joined herself to it; did Sanctuary need to be sentient as well? And if so, how on earth was I supposed to do that? All I could sense was vague, gentle light.

I stretched further. Something soft brushed against my awareness—feathers or fur. Then nothing but more golden light.

Scott said the Valley had been leeching his life, using his life to feed itself.

A tiny seed of fear surfaced through the peace and calm of the golden light. I swallowed hard. It made sense. It was logical. And I couldn't think of anything else to try. I had no way to catch the light, no way to drag it to Gemma; I needed it alive so that it could be persuaded to do it itself.

This... was going to hurt.

Gritting my teeth, I turned my road mastery upon myself. I couldn't see my own soulprint of course, but I knew where it was, and I could sense that I was there, alive, a thing, a source of life. Slowly, one tiny piece at a time, I drew on that life force, reeling it out into my road mastery. It didn't hurt as much as I'd feared; it felt a little like using shadow magic.

When I thought I had enough balled up to make a start, I pushed it further out, away from me, away from my road master sense, and feeding it into the light of Sanctuary's heart.

I winced. Okay, so that part hurt. A lot. It felt like I was tugging on a nerve connected deep inside my body, one sharp, shooting pulse of pain that travelled out into the light ahead of me. But Sanctuary was responding; the flutter of feather and fur brushed against my road mastery again, more solid this time, more real. *Come on*, I told it. *Take it. Take my life force.*

It nibbled tentatively—at least, that's what it felt like, tiny bumping contacts like a small, toothless fish.

Slowly, carefully, I fed out some more. Each breath tore raggedly at my throat, and my chest burned like a needle of molten lead had been stabbed through it.

But it was working. A shape took form in front of me: wings; knobbly, golden-furred legs; liquid brown eyes; a glorious golden mane.

I felt it staring at me, curiosity burning in its gaze. *Not me,* I told it. *Gemma. You have to talk to Gemma.*

Its gaze shifted. I fed it more life and it solidified as I watched: a winged horse, small, but growing steadily. It took a cautious step toward Gemma—I could vaguely sense her soulprint in that direction, and I encouraged the horse as vigorously as I could. *Yes. Yes, that's it. Help her. You have to help her.*

It snorted, tossed its mane—and stepped toward her.

The pain in my chest crushed me. Somehow I could see my own fingers beneath my eyes, and they were vague and insubstantial. But the horse, the horse was glorious and real and it was going to Gemma, and she was raising a hand to greet it like an old friend. *Yes*.

Tired. So, so tired. I lay down on the floor.

The pain was nearly gone. I just needed to rest for a moment. Then I'd be fine.

Gemma laughed.

I'd missed that sound so much.

She stood up, strong and vibrant. The black tether of the Valley rippled into her soulprint—and directly opposite, a strong, golden cord anchored her to Sanctuary, fine tendrils creeping through her soulprint and binding it back together.

I smiled, and the last of my tension melted away. We'd done it. Gemma was going to be safe.

The horse's great wings flapped. It whipped toward me. Distantly, I saw fear cross Gemma's face. But it didn't matter, because I'd saved her. *I won't forget you*, I promised Gemma. *Never. Tell Mum and Dad I love them. Anna too.*

Gemma's face crumpled. "No! Emma!"

Don't look back, I thought, smiling. *Don't say goodbye. It's okay.*

"Emma, wait! Emma! Don't do this! Emma, no!"

I closed my eyes; every muscle in my body relaxed. I'd done it. It had worked.

I'd saved Gemma, and everything would be well.

Soft violin strings plucking. The gentle motion of a river rocking me to sleep. The smell of blue.

"Emma, no!"

I could barely hear her now. Colours washed around me, soft rain pattering, glowing warmth surrounding me.

Every sense in my body was alive, so much more alive than I'd ever been before, and as I gave in and drifted, I felt myself break away from everything negative, from every doubt, every fear. I floated, blissful, drunk on golden light and peaceful warmth. If this was death, I thought, it was magical, and no one on Earth should be afraid of it.

22

I FELL BACKWARD into nothingness, and everything around me turned gold and warm and soft. For minutes, hours, years, I lost myself in the comfort and beauty of it all, drifting gently on a stream of eternal happiness.

After what might have been centuries, I bumped against something solid—a seed, a kernel, a nut— and it shifted and shook. Touching it seemed like the most natural thing in the world, and as I did, blood from my finger smeared the nut and blackened its shell. Black and gold, life and death.

Green began to grow.

The seed kernel sprouted and twisted and grew, and I saw visions above me of a green land sprouting, light and dark and green blending together in perfect harmony, and I understood: once, the hearts had been bound together. And once, the lands above them had been bound together in harmony too; no Valley, no Sanctuary, just one wide land stretching from sea to mountain ridges, bright and shining and glorious.

Suddenly, I realised I was drawing closer to the representation of Sanctuary stretched over me. Underneath me something stretched and bunched, stretched and bunched, and beside me great wings beat.

Golden wings. Golden soft feathers, and underneath me, golden soft hair; in my hands, long strands—a mane.

A neck, ears and a head; a pegasus horse, brighter than the sun, more golden than ingots, warm as a winter fire.

And in front of us, a golden cord, connecting us to the image of Sanctuary—to a great, pulsing heart, gold and glowing.

We drew closer and closer to the great ball of gold that shone like the sun, and as we drew near, two patches of darkness appeared within the glow, one a starry night with the deep velvet warmth of summer, and one the dark starlight cold of winter— my two best friends.

We flew like an arrow toward them, and around me the dream shattered, and the vision of the land above me dissolved away and everything was gold and warm, pulsing with the wingbeats of the pegasus I rode.

Then abruptly we were in the chamber of Sanctuary's heart, and the Pegasus jerked downward for a moment as weight redistributed.

Arms wrapped around my waist and somebody sobbed against my shoulder.

"I thought you were dead. I thought you were dead!"

Something sparkled in front of us, and before I could figure out what it was, it shattered over us like cold glass, shivering down my spine and through my hair, and then we were flashing forward through time, rainbows arching around us, clouds forming and dissipating, sounds barely hitting my eardrums before we left them behind again as we sped onward, onward, onward.

I held onto Gemma's arms fiercely and cried and laughed and cried because I'd saved her, and she was okay, and the avatar of Sanctuary was a big, beautiful pegasus, and he was flying us home, home, home.

23

WE LANDED ON the beach in Sanctuary, and as we tumbled off the pegasus, we stared around.

"What happened?" Gemma whispered.

Around us, the beach lay cracked and broken. Further on, pine trees stood at crazy angles, some leaning against their neighbours, some snapped and lying on the ground. "It must have been the earthquakes," I replied quietly. But the elation I'd had at surviving, at saving Gem, was sorely rattled. What had we done?

Behind me was still, too still. I turned.

Scott.

I shifted myself around to face him. "Are you okay?"

His face was sharp, eyes narrow, jaw tight, and his gaze slid off the side of my face and landed in the middle distance. "I'm okay."

I fought the urge to just collapse, right there in the sand. All this—*all this*—and now it seemed like maybe Scott was mad at me. "Are you sure?"

For a long moment, I thought he wouldn't answer. A breeze drifted in off the ocean, bearing salt and clean air. I breathed deeply, appreciating the smell of being alive. The roads had been incredible, but at least here I could focus on one sensation at a time. I inhaled again, savouring the smell of salty air and vowing to never forget it.

"You nearly died," Scott said, and suddenly I had the full attention of his gaze, and it was weighty.

I shrugged. "I guess." I remembered feeding my life force into the heart of Sanctuary... My gaze flicked quickly toward the great golden pegasus. "I called it to life," I said without meaning to. *Wow*, I thought, staring at it. The pegasus. Sanctuary's avatar. I'd brought it to life. I blinked rapidly and shook my head a little. *Wow*.

"That was stupid."

The cruelty in Scott's voice sent a chill of discomfort through my chest. "I had to," I said, facing him again. "It was the only way to save Gemma."

"You didn't have to. I thought we'd talked about you not dying for her sake."

I turned my attention back to him, bristling. "It wasn't like I sat there and had a philosophical discussion about it before I did it, you know. It was the only thing I could do at the time, so I did it. And it worked! I saved her!"

Scott stared out at the ocean again, hands fisting. "You nearly died!"

Sadness and frustration welled in my chest. I clenched my teeth, tossing my head to stop the tears before they could start. "But I didn't, so I don't know why you're so upset! It's all fine! What is your *problem*?!"

That weighty gaze again, pinning me in place.

I refused to squirm.

"Really?" he said, softly, but full of something dark, something heavy—regret? Anger? "You can't see what really happened?"

I frowned. "What—" I cut off and squinted at him. Something... Something else was going on here. Something in the way he sat, or looked, or sounded...

Oh. I sat back, eyes wide. *Oh.*

He nodded fractionally. "So you do see it. I thought you must."

I reached hesitantly for him with my road mastery wide, wide open so I could examine his newly-changed soulprint. "Does... Did it hurt?"

He shrugged. "No. Actually it was pretty nice, compared to the Valley."

I ran my fingers down the side of his face, right where I could see his soulprint glowing—because now instead of cold, vast starlight on the top of a darkened mountain, Scott's soulprint glowed gold: the same mountain top, the same vast sense of distance, but now a dawning, the blush of sunrise on the horizon burning away the stars and filling up the darkness. "What did you do?"

He turned away sharply, breaking contact with my fingers. "You were dying."

I was dying. I'd fed all my life-force into the heart of Sanctuary, and I'd left nothing in reserve for myself. I was dying, and he'd come to save me. "What did you do?" I repeated, softer this time.

"The same as I did for the Valley. I... submitted to it. Let it draw on my life force. The same thing you did," he added, eyebrows quirking upward as he glanced at me.

"But how did you know what to do? That I was dying?" How did you wake up in time? I didn't add, remembering him just starting to stir as I'd begun that final stage of the journey.

His breathing was too fast, his fingertips white as he gripped his biceps. He rocked back and forth, once, twice, then doubled over, right down to his knees, and drew in a great, shuddering breath.

I reached for him, but he lifted his head and met my eye. "I knew, because I'd done it once before. Only that time I was too slow, and she died right in front of me."

My stomach did complicated things, and this time I didn't even try to stop the tears from making shining tracks down my cheeks. "But this time, it worked," I said quietly—so quietly. "I'm not dead, Scott. You saved me. Thank you."

He drew in a long, shaky breath. "Yeah. So we're even now, okay?" He said it lightly, but the way his hands fisted at his sides betrayed the weight of it.

I half-smiled, half-sighed, and rubbed away my tears. "Yeah," I said. "I guess we are."

The waves shushed in against the sand. When we'd first arrived, before the roads, it had felt like they were asking a question: Where? Where? Where? I still had the lingering sense of questioning, but the focus seemed to have shifted: When? When? When?

"So..." I said, facing Scott again. "We're all connected to Sanctuary now?"

He shrugged. "Ask it." He tilted his head at the pegasus, who had turned and was regarding us curiously.

I swallowed. "Are... Wait." I scrunched up my face and shook my head. "What do we call you?" I asked the pegasus.

It bowed, head touched to one bent knee. "Helios," it said. "For I am the sun."

I bowed my head in return. "Uh, I'm... Edge. And this is... Scott?"

Helios tossed his head. "I know who you are. You are the ones who gave me life, and for this, I thank you."

I glanced at Scott, then licked my lips. "Are... Are we still giving you life? I mean, are we still connected to you now?"

"He is," Helios said. "You are not. You nearly gave me too much as it was. I tried to break the connection with you, but you had given me life and so it was like trying to separate myself from myself; I could not do it." He bowed his head, sad or thoughtful or maybe both. "But Scott, he was able to assist. Our connection is stable. It is slow. I will not draw his life away from him. You gave me too much, Edge," Helios added solemnly. "It would not have been good for you to die in order to give me life."

Not you, I didn't have the courage to say. Not you.

I took Gemma by the hand, and Scott took my free hand, and together we led our newfound avatar back to Sanctuary—to his home.

24

WE HEADED BACK toward Sanctuary, uncertain of what we would find. The land was quiet and empty, like it was sleeping—or maybe recovering. On the other side of the line of trees, we all paused in shock: a giant chasm had opened, separating the meadow from the entrance alcove.

Mrs Caro and Aphros appeared at the stables, and as soon as they spotted us, came hurrying over. There were hugs all round—even for Scott—and then we arranged ourselves in some sort of cluster and headed back to the stables.

"The twins are fine," Mrs Caro told us.

"I thank you for your assistance," Aphros said, bowing her head solemnly at Mrs Caro.

There was a really great story there, at some point.

My jaw cracked as I yawned. Yep. At some point.

"So," I said as we reached the stables. "What are our chances of being allowed in Sanctuary again, now that we're all connected to its avatar?"

Aphros snorted. "If that fairy of yours has her way, I would judge them to be extremely high."

"*Our* fairy."

"She was not like this until she met you, that much is certain," Aphros said, and through our connection I could sense her amusement.

I pulled a face at her.

"Look, here she comes now," Mrs Caro said, pointing upslope as Quoise sped toward us.

"You're alive!" Quoise squealed as she joined us, flying in a whirling circle, surveying first Gemma, then Scott, then me. She turned to Helios and bowed in the air. "Greetings, denizen of Sanctuary. You are welcome here."

"Greetings, Keeper of the Heart," Helios replied, bowing also.

I raised both eyebrows.

Gem giggled. "She's not the Keeper."

Mrs Caro, Aphros and Quoise exchanged glances.

"What?" I demanded. "What's going on?"

Mrs Caro cleared her throat. "She challenged the leadership of Sanctuary."

Quoise grinned madly. "By the book," she said. "No wonder Viri hid the Book of Law. Not that I've been accepted," Quoise added quickly. "My claim is based mostly on the fact that Viri has been lying to everyone to hold onto her power, but not everyone believes me, and lot of them still believe *her*."

Mrs Caro nodded. "I can't imagine them appreciating the implication that the Valley and Sanctuary used to be connected."

Quoise snorted. "Not so much, no."

"But why?" I asked.

Scott answered, plunging his hands into their usual place in his pockets. "Fear of the Valley," he said simply. He stared at me, but when I remained confused, he continued. "If the fairies stay scared of the Valley, she holds onto her power. But if there's even a hint that the Valley used to be part of Sanctuary, it means the Valley isn't evil—it's something they can fix. *Pfft* goes her control."

Quoise nodded. "Exactly."

I rubbed my hands over my face. "Okay. So, what do we do about it?"

"First," Mrs Caro said very firmly, taking first my hand, then Gemma's, and indicating with her head for Scott to join the line. He did, and she inclined her head approvingly. "Good. First what we're going to do is this."

I waited eagerly for her plan of action, pleased not to be the one concocting it for a change.

"We're going to have this wonderful pegasus here fly us down to the alcove, and then we're going to go home, all of us. And then we're going to have hot showers, and a good meal, and we're going to sleep. *All* of us. For a long time. And then, in a few days, when everyone is feeling better and we've gotten used to all of these recent *changes*..." She eyed us all significantly. "Well, then perhaps we can meet together and decide what—if anything—we should do about this."

Part of me was disappointed with her advice— but a larger, more sensible part of me was really, really *tired*. How many hours had I been up now? A rest sounded really, really good. So did dinner and a hot shower.

And a few days without worrying about friends dying or about saving the world? That sounded like the absolute best of all.

So we held hands, and Mrs Caro got us back to Earth before eight, and as we pushed our way through the tea tree scrub and past sweeping eucalyptus boughs to the crunching gravel of the path, I lifted my face to the dark, cloudy skies of home and breathed deeply, because my friends were safe, and my family was safe. And even when the clouds broke as I headed up the steps through the boulders toward home, I laughed, because the raindrops were fresh and cold and electric, and they washed everything away.

I walked through my back gate and into the house, and there was Dad in his armchair reading, and Anna's music blared from her room and Veve's tail thump-thump-thumped on the floor before she got up and came to greet me, and Mum was in the kitchen baking cookies.

"How's Gem?" she asked, raising her head sharply as I entered, and I laughed, and hugged her, because we'd made it, and I'd saved Gemma, and Scott had saved me, and everything was perfectly, brilliantly fine.

THANK YOU!

Dear You,

Thank you for taking the time to read this book! I hope you enjoyed reading it as much as I enjoyed making it. It was fun digging into the background of the characters some more, and I think all the Scott-fans out there should be pleased ;)

If you *did* like it, and you'd like to see more *Sanctuary* books, please consider leaving a review wherever you bought this book, or on Amazon, or GoodReads, or on your school or work noticeboard, or scrawled on your best friend's hand. Probably not their face. That would be a little cruel. But anywhere else works, really. It's the fact that you recommended it to someone that matters.

(Also don't use blood. You don't want to end up in the Valley, do you? No. I didn't think so.)

Anyway, if you made it this far, you are genuinely amazing, and I love and adore you. YOU are what makes writing books worthwhile. Thank you :3

Love and unicorns,
Amy

WANT TO KNOW MORE?

Sign up for Amy's mailing list to be notified of new releases, sales, cover reveals—and for the chance to win a free copy of each book she releases!

http://www.amylaurens.com/about/mailing-list

ACKNOWLEDGEMENTS

With thanks to Liana, who kept me sane, Daimien, who kept me fed, and every single person who let me know that they enjoyed book one, and wanted to know when book two would be out. You guys kept me going through some pretty in-frogging-sane deadlines on this one. Phew.

Further thanks are also due to Kimberly, Bethy, Shanna, Miles and Bethany, for their invaluable assistance in pointing out errors. Any remaining mistakes are, of course, all mine.

Clare also deserves a mention for dealing with my constantly-in-flux-but-always-pressing deadlines; your patience and adaptability = awesomeness, and the cover is simply glorious.

Anthea for naming Filibere (though I took some liberties, sorry) and Lily for unwittingly donating her name—Lily, your enthusiasm at the signing for *Where Shadows Rise* that night at Harry Hartog's was utterly inspiring. Thank you so much.

And lastly, my parents, who instilled in me the unshakeable belief that I am saved. Thanks <3

ABOUT THE AUTHOR

AMY LAURENS is an Australian author of fantasy fiction for all ages. She has never seen a fairy or travelled to Sanctuary (sadly), but she has definitely owned a Labrador almost exactly like Veve (though Amy's Labrador was yellow, not brown).

And while she's definitely not a Road Master (pity), her kids are pretty sure she has eyes in the back of her head and a sixth sense for spotting trouble. She hasn't told anyone this, but actually she has *two* sets of eyes in the back of her head—one because she's a mum, and one because she's a teacher.

You can find out more about Amy at her website, www.amylaurens.com.